Jeopardy in January

A Calendar Mystery

USA TODAY Bestselling Author
CAMILLA CHAFER

ALSO BY CAMILLA CHAFER

CHAPTER ONE

"I'm going to save this library if it's the last thing I do!" I declared, raising my fist emphatically in the air. I looked around at the empty library. Unfortunately, my rallying cry wasn't exactly drawing in the troops, unless the troops consisted of me and my colleague, Bree Shaw.

"Okay, but are you going to save it while wearing the Supergirl outfit? Or do you plan to go home and change first?" asked Bree. She wrinkled her nose as she looked up at me and shook her head.

Looking down at the shiny blue leotard, red mini skirt and long, red boots edged in gold, I winced. I knew I looked ridiculous. Standing on a chair, my fist stretched to the ceiling, I continued trying to rally Bree at the end of a very long day. It was a special day for Calendar Middle School: a visit from the Superheroes-in-Fiction day. I insisted we both dress the part and instantly regretted it. January weather wasn't suited to shiny Spandex.

With a long sigh, I lowered my fist as I climbed down. "I think I might change first," I said, trying to ignore Bree's stifled laughter. "But I definitely intend to come up with a successful plan. The town needs this library. We can't let them take it away!"

"They aren't exactly taking it away," Bree pointed out. With her hand on the chair I was stepping down from, she waited until both of my feet were on the ground before tucking it under the antique desk that served as the hub of the library. The desk had probably been there as long as the library. It may even have been older and I loved it. The intricately carved legs and old runners that held two very deep drawers, along with the lightly scratched cherrywood top that saw countless books pass over it during the decades of service, had become a fixture. It even had my name, *Sara Cutler*, proudly printed on a metal strip above my job title: *Librarian*. I didn't love the desk quite as much as I loved the library because the old building was something else indeed.

One of the first buildings to be established in Calendar, the library had an interesting and unique history. Beautifully built, it had two floors, and still retained the original, carved double doors. Above the entry was a circular window that beamed in light through the stained-glass depiction of a book held by childlike hands. Inside was the most stunning, wrought iron spiral staircase. I once bravely mounted the banister and slid all the way down. The walls held shelf after shelf of old and new books, with dozens of freestanding racks in between. It was literally stuffed with a large variety of reading material.

Upstairs was reserved for the non-fiction and a small rare books section, many tomes bequeathed from local residents for the pleasure of new generations. Downstairs belonged to the fiction, and a large square was separated by a partition and dedicated purely to children's books. The children's section was peppered with low tables and little, wooden chairs, as well as a stack of soft, colorful, seating mats, their covers crocheted by the Calendar Craft Club.

The library was as beautiful inside as it was outside. Set onto a large corner plot, it boasted a large, rambling garden. Over the years, it had become a favorite spot for teddy bear picnics and summer book clubs.

Unfortunately, the size of the plot was now part of the current problem. It cost a large percentage of the library's small funds to maintain the garden as well as the building, and it was also a very attractive lot to outside investors. Several building development offers had been previously knocked back by the town council... until now.

"I know they want to move it but they... they simply can't!" I spluttered loudly. I tried to imagine the library being bulldozed and replaced with a cul-de-sac of cookie cutter homes. "Everyone loves the library!"

"Don't look now, but that guy doesn't," said Bree. She gave a small nod of her head toward the front doors. "I better check the children's section," she added as she moved away quickly.

I noted the draft when the doors opened but ignored it. Now I saw they were closed again to the cold, snowy weather and my stomach dropped. The man in front of the doors had a sprinkle of snow on his short brown hair and expensive wool coat with the collar turned up. He definitely didn't endorse my desire to save the library. No, Jason Rees wanted to relocate all of the books into a faceless, character-less building on the other side of town, and knock down the library, so he could build a tract of non-descript homes on the prime real estate.

I watched him open the door again before he shook his umbrella outside. When he closed it, I saw him press it firmly as if he'd only just noticed the door's tendency to stick in the colder months. Looking around as if he were visiting for the first time, he left the umbrella in the antique stand by the door. I had no doubt that he already knew where the stand was and had come here merely to assess the area.

If he actually came here for that, it probably meant he was also checking to see if I were working.

I couldn't blame him. After all, Jason Rees and I didn't get off to the best start when he arrived two weeks ago. He glibly informed me the library was closing before my boss even had a chance to tell me. My cheeks still burned every time I recalled my reaction. I told him to get out while yelling at him loudly, and then I called my boss. She listened to my complaint about the "city upstart" before she confirmed the news. It turned out to be the worst day of my career! The past two weeks only continued to become difficult. Jason stopped by several times, either with architects or the foreman, or to deliver more unpleasant news. I couldn't fault him for his good manners, and effortless charm, but the nicer he got, the more irked I became.

Turning away, I searched for something to busy myself with, wanting to appear as if I hadn't already noticed Jason. I picked up a couple of books and added them to the trolley, which Bree would later return to their proper shelves. When he didn't approach my desk after a couple of minutes with my back turned, I couldn't resist stealing a quick glance over my shoulder.

Jason wasn't there!

I turned all the way around, frowning as I scanned the room. Where the hell was he?

Eyeing the grandfather clock—a gift to the library from an elderly patron more than forty years ago—I saw there was only ten minutes until closing time. I really didn't want to spend that time looking for Jason. It would have been a lot better if he just approached my desk, told me the day's awful news regarding the library, and then got lost. Preferably, straight into a torrential snow shower; one that would stop the moment I stepped out of the library!

"The children's section is all cleared up," said Bree. She added a small stack of books to the trolley. "I also passed out a pamphlet to everyone to encourage them to join the library if they haven't already."

"Great! The kids all received their bookmarks too?" I asked.

"Yes, for the third time, and I gave each of them a program of events. That way, they can include their families too for all the upcoming events you organized. I think the summer family book club will be quite popular."

"Good thinking, Bree," I praised her.

"So what did you-know-who want?" she asked, pulling a face.

"I have no idea." I looked past Bree to the umbrella stand. Yep, his umbrella was still there, and dripping obnoxiously. "He didn't come over to see me. I'm not sure where he is now."

"Do you want me to find him and show him the door?" Bree asked helpfully. She tried to appear as defiant as she could while wearing a Winnie-the-Pooh plush costume, complete with hood and ears. I wondered how that fitted in with the superhero theme but Bree insisted Pooh was a hero (of sorts) and besides, all the kids liked it.

"No, it's okay, I'll do it. You can go home though if you want. It looks like the snow might have lessened a little bit and I don't think anyone else will venture in today. Plus, the weather report said we're due a rain storm that will wash away the snow so the weather might get nasty very soon. I'll show Jason to the door and lock it behind him."

"Don't let it hit him on the ass on his way out," Bree advised me as she wriggled out of the costume before wedging it into a plastic bag. Reaching under the desk, she grabbed her purse, and waved as she walked over to the coat rack by the door and picked off her thick, winter coat. She slipped out the door quickly and pulled the door closed.

I looked around, sweeping as much of the library with my eyes as I could from the desk. There didn't appear to be anyone else in the building. Then I heard the sound of footsteps crossing the upstairs floor. Jason was definitely still here; and for some unfathomable reason, he was upstairs.

I switched off the computer—Jason definitely hadn't come here to borrow a book—and while it powered down, I grabbed the keys from the drawer. I went over to the front door, flipping the lock so no one else could wander in and prevent me from escaping home. After a day on my feet, I planned a relaxing evening, comprised of dinner for one, a hot bath, and a good book. The only obstacle that stood between that and me now was Jason.

I headed for the staircase, wondering what he was doing up there. Probably admiring the view of the gardens and calculating how many homes he could squeeze onto the lot.

The second floor had a horseshoe shape, and the three sides held iron railings that enabled people to look downstairs, while the fourth opened onto the staircase. On a bright, sunny day, the stained-glass porthole window cast a pretty pattern on the stairs. Today, however, was almost non-stop snow and the dark sky was filled with clouds.

The upstairs layout allowed me to very easily see people no matter where they were, and as I ascended the staircase, I was grateful. It could save me some time today. Jason was standing in front of the rear windows with his back to me and looking out into the dim light of the garden. I instantly concluded he must have been surveying the lot while working out his profit and loss in acquiring the land and selling the subsequent homes to prospective residents, or whatever nefarious means property developers followed.

"We're closing now," I called out when I was only a few feet away.

Jason turned, his face looking blank before he blinked, and I wondered if I surprised him. One glance at the expensive watch peeking out from under his navy cashmere sweater was enough for me to deduce it was probably worth more than two, maybe even three, months of my salary. Landmark demolition and subsequent property development must be a lucrative business. "They already told you?" he asked without preamble, fixing his blue eyes sternly on mine.

"What?" I frowned.

"That a date has been set."

"Wait... what?" I frowned harder.

Jason produced an envelope from the inside pocket of his jacket and handed it to me. The flap wasn't stuck so I inserted my thumb and flipped it open before pulling out the single sheet of folded paper. I scanned it quickly, my frown only deepening further.

"What is this?"

"It's an eviction notice, and part of the agreement of the pre-sale negotiations. My firm sent me here to serve it on behalf..."

"I can see that!" I snapped, cutting him off rudely, but I didn't care. "It says we have to pack up and be out in two weeks! The building isn't even sold yet!"

"The landlord shared the details of the most recent building inspection with my firm. The roof is showing obvious signs of leakage and the windows need replacing. The garden is neglected and overgrown. They can't afford to keep this place up any longer so they're shutting it down until the escrow closes and they're no longer responsible."

Rage shook me. "You can't do this!"

"It's already been done. Listen, Sara, I'm really sorry. I know this library means a lot to you but we made a deal and Calendar will get a new library, a much better one." The hopeful smile faltered.

"We want *this* library." My utter shock rooted me to the spot.

"Why? It's just a building."

"It isn't *just a building*!" Taking a deep breath, I was well aware that I should have been shushing myself and not raising my voice. "Look around," I said, sweeping a hand through the air, wondering if Jason could even see what I saw. "You seem to think this is just an old building. I see a living history, the beating heart of this town! Almost every single resident has entered this library at some point in their lives. Old people that came here as kids are now bringing their grandkids. We advance literacy in the community. We host events and provide books to seniors. We keep the population entertained and inspired. It isn't just a useless building! And not something you can sacrifice and tear down just to throw up another bunch of faceless, generic houses."

"They won't be faceless or generic! And besides, Calendar needs new homes," Jason added quickly. "It's a beautiful town so consequently, lots of people would love to raise their families here. They need to live somewhere."

"I know but not where *this* library stands."

"The sale is still going through." Jason glanced back at the garden and I thought I glimpsed something sad, almost regretful, in his eyes. No! I must have been mistaken. Jason Rees was an unfeeling property developer. He didn't care about old buildings, or even new ones. All he cared about was profit. Arguing with him any longer was a waste of my breath.

"I still have two weeks, right?" I inquired.

He nodded. "Two weeks. We'll send someone to help you with all the packing and moving. That's included in the deal too," he said, his voice gentler. I expected him to be harsher.

"But we have two weeks," I pressed. "And then the library will be sold?"

"Yes."

I smiled, remembering what I said to Bree only twenty minutes ago. "I'm going to save the library," I valiantly told him, pushing my shoulders back and standing up as tall as I could. Jason might have been a tall man, and easily six inches taller than me, but I endowed myself with stature and presence.

Jason's lips quirked into a smile as he raked in a long look from head to toe and back up again. I saw a smile quivering at the edges of his lips. "Sure, Supergirl," he said, stepping around me and making for the exit.

I frowned at his comment, only realizing what he meant when I looked down. My costume! I groaned as I smacked my palm against my forehead. How embarrassing! Not only did he fail to see why the town needed the library but he also assumed I must be pretty pathetic too. Bree was right! I should have gone home and changed first. At least, it might have spared me that humiliation.

After I heard the door bang shut, I followed Jason's path downstairs, stomping on every stair out of annoyance. Snatching my winter coat off the rack, I switched off the lights on the panel by the door and stepped outside, pulling the door shut. I had to do it once and then again, which resulted in a bang because of its nasty habit of sticking in cold weather. I locked it with the old, heavy key, which I then deposited in my pocket.

Zipping my coat over my costume, I shivered. The snow grew heavier throughout the afternoon and barely let up. The brief reprieve of a few minutes ago apparently was over. "I should have kicked Jason out and left with Bree," I muttered to myself. Instead of being cozy in my thick jacket and knit hat, I fully expected to feel like a drowned rat by the time I got home. At least the pleasure of a hot bath and a good book while I soaked still awaited me.

Ten frozen minutes into the walk, I realized my purse wasn't on my arm. I knew it was still under the desk. Inside was not only the book I planned to read but even worse, my house keys! After being first distracted by Jason, and then humiliated by my costume, I'd forgotten to collect my purse before I left.

Sheltering under the cover of a tree, I looked back in the direction of the library, quickly calculating the options. I could walk back ten minutes and get my purse, and then walk the twenty minutes it took to return home, which meant I would be spending a total of thirty more minutes in the snow. Or I could continue home for ten more minutes and look forward to a very boring evening as well as an embarrassing phone call to my mom to ask for my spare keys. I sighed at my conundrum. I really wanted to read that book. The last chapter was a cliffhanger and now, there was no way I could wait until tomorrow's lunch break to find out who was stalking the heroine. Plus, taking a hot bath when I got home would certainly steam off the extra exposure to snow. More importantly though, I wouldn't have to call my mom and make her come out in the cold before enduring a lecture from her that if I could find a nice man, then someone else would have a spare key.

My mind made up, I turned back, walking double-time on my return trip to the library. Halfway, the snow stopped. The sidewalk, slick with snow and ice, was slippery and as I made the turn, I glided on the dark path leading to the library doors. I was temporarily forced to slow down as I pulled my keys from my pocket.

On the threshold, I stopped dead, slurries of snow sloshing my ankles. The door hung slightly open, and icy water was pooling on the parquet floor inside. *Did I forget to lock the door?* I tried to remember as I pushed it open. No, I definitely locked it! I'd been careful because the door stuck and I remembered turning the key while my cheeks still burned at the thought of Jason raking a look over me in the tight Supergirl costume.

"Bree?" I called as I stepped inside, flicking on the lights and illuminating the racks. Only Bree had the other set of keys. Perhaps in her hurry to leave, she forgot something, just like I did? "Bree, are you still here?" I called out again, louder this time.

No answer.

From upstairs came a muffled thud.

"Bree?" I called again, walking a few steps further inside. Worry churned my stomach. It was that uncomfortable gut feeling I invariably got when something was awfully, horribly wrong. Having only had that feeling a few times in my life, here it was again, and instantly recognizable. Was Bree in trouble? Had she hurt herself in the snow and stumbled back here?

I walked towards the stairs, slowly going up, my heart rate racing. I couldn't see Bree as I walked around. "Bree?" I called again, more worried now. What if the thud weren't from Bree? What if someone else were inside? Images of violence raced through my head. Who would break into the library? There weren't a lot of valuable items inside. The computer system was ancient and cranky. The grandfather clock would require two or more men and a truck to transport. The only thing worth stealing was a particularly good collection of mystery paperbacks.

I stopped at the top of the staircase and something caught my eye.

A foot was barely visible in the rare books section, and the leather ankle boot seemed awfully familiar. I admired the style several times. Rushing forwards, I kept trying to ignore my mounting fear.

The foot was attached to a leg.

The leg was definitely part of a prone body.

I stopped, a terrified cry rising in my throat. Blood pooled from a head that was turned away from me, and the tumbling, dark brown hair lay limp on the floor.

I screamed, only for it to be cut off when a large pair of arms closed around me.

CHAPTER TWO

"How well did you know the victim?"

I looked up, blinking with the vaguest recollection that it wasn't the first time Detective Logan had asked me that question. This time, I forced the words into my dry mouth. "Not well. Bree only worked at the library for three months," I told him.

"Were you friends?"

"Yes."

"What can you tell me about her?"

"She had an apartment on Oak Street. She was twenty-seven years old, same age as me, and she..." I stopped. I wanted to say something else about Bree but when I scrabbled around in my mind for something significant to tell the detective, I realized I didn't know anything! I could describe some things about Bree; I could tell him her height, her hair, her eye color and how she liked her coffee, but I couldn't actually tell him anything about her. I didn't know anything. How could that be true? "I don't know," I said, cringing at how lame I sounded.

"You don't know anything about your friend?" asked Detective Logan. He raised a hand to his forehead, brushing back the snow. His hair was so dark red, it was a handsome shade of auburn. His green eyes watched me.

"I, uh..."

The hand holding mine squeezed me reassuringly and I suddenly remembered how long we'd been holding hands. *Far longer than necessary,* I thought, *even if he was warm*. "She's in shock," said Jason. "Shock makes it hard for a person to concentrate on any details. Sara just found her friend dead."

Detective Logan turned his suspicious eyes on Jason. The two men were the same height, forcing me to look up at them as they continued their stare-off. "And you are?"

"Jason Rees. I'm with the property management firm redeveloping the lot the library sits on."

"Uh-huh." Detective Logan gave him a long look but I couldn't decide if he were annoyed at that snippet of news or just puzzled. "And you're here… because?"

"I was driving past the library when I saw someone running out. The door was wide open and I knew it was past closing time so that was odd too. It was highly unlikely that anyone would have left the door open in this weather so I thought I should check it out."

"Did you get a good look at this person?"

Jason shook his head. "No."

"Why not?"

"Because it was dark and snowing!" Jason sounded exasperated. "I think it was a man. He was almost as tall as me and as broad, but I wasn't expecting to give anyone a witness description later."

"Maybe it's a good job you turned up when you did," said Detective Logan, shooting a sideways glance at me. I shivered.

"I guess," said Jason.

"Sara could have been hurt too."

"I know," said Jason with a worried expression.

"I didn't see anyone inside," I told them. I didn't dare to imagine what could have befallen me if Jason hadn't arrived when he did. I was sure I heard someone moving upstairs, but I was also sure now that it couldn't have been Bree.

"Are you positive about that?"

"Yes. I didn't see anyone. I thought I heard a thud upstairs though."

"Could it have been Bree?"

"I don't think so. She looked..." I trailed off and Detective Logan nodded knowingly.

"It could have been creaks in the old building or the footsteps of her killer," said Detective Logan. "She hasn't been dead very long."

A wave of nausea washed over me at the thought. Had I really been so close to a murderer? Was he still in the library when I came through the door? What if I'd been here a few minutes earlier? And what if Jason hadn't turned up when he did? I couldn't help screaming when I saw Bree's body, and that was almost the exact same moment Jason grabbed hold of me. I screamed again then until I realized who it was. He got one look at

Bree before he practically carried me out of the library, comforting me and holding me close to him as he phoned the police.

That brought up two more questions. Why did Bree return to the library? And why was Jason hanging around?

"I don't know why she was even there still," I said, and my jaw started to tremble as the cold seeped through me. Jason took the blanket the EMTs draped over my shoulders and tucked it in before wrapping an arm around me. His other hand returned to lace his fingers with mine. If someone had told me two weeks ago that we would be locking fingers, I would have told them crossly that it would never happen! However, now it was strangely comforting. I just hoped I wouldn't burst into tears on him.

"She wasn't locking the doors?" asked Detective Logan.

I quickly shook my head. "No. Bree left ten minutes before I did and I locked up. I definitely locked the door behind me because it sticks and I had to pull it hard. She shouldn't have been there."

"Should you have been there at that time?"

I shook my head. "No, I should have been home already. But I was in such a hurry to get home in the snow that I forgot my purse. I had to go back and get it."

"So Bree could have forgotten something too?"

"I don't know. Maybe. She had her purse on her though when she left. I remember seeing that," I said, shivering.

"Did she have a key to the library?"

"Yes, she opens it every morning."

"Could she have been there for any other reason?"

"C'mon on, Detective! Can't you see Sara is in shock? I should take her home! She shouldn't be standing out here in the cold, answering endless questions. She's shivering! She needs a hot drink right now and some warm, dry, clothes."

Detective Logan studied Jason, and then, me. "How long have you two been together?" he asked.

"We're not!" I squeaked in protest. I shivered again and pushed back a damp strand from my forehead. Despite Jason's umbrella, it could not shield us from the onslaught of snow, and my hair was dripping wet. Perhaps I should have taken up the EMT's offer to sit inside their van.

Detective Logan looked down at our intertwined hands and nodded, clearly full of disbelief. Color spread across my cheeks. I pulled my hand out of Jason's and stuck it in my pocket. "How are you getting home?" asked Detective Logan.

"I usually walk. My house isn't too far and it's never worth driving."

"I'll drive her," said Jason. "My car is just over there." He pointed to a black SUV across the street, the only vehicle not confined by the ambulance or patrol cars.

"Just so long as you don't try to fly," said Detective Logan, nodding to my costume, which he managed to glimpse from under my coat. I suppressed a sigh as I resolved to burn the costume just as soon as I could. It was fast becoming the source of far too much amusement for the adult population of Calendar, and a total embarrassment for me, even if the kids liked it. "I'll need to question you, possibly at length, again. Both of you," he added. "Don't leave town until then, Mr. Rees."

"Am I a suspect?" asked Jason, sounding surprised.

"Should you be?" countered Detective Logan, his eyebrows rising.

"No."

"Stick around anyway," he said in a warning tone before he turned away, leaving the pair of us alone.

"You don't have to drive me home," I told Jason. I shrugged off the blanket from the EMT and dropped it into the nearby ambulance. Jason followed me with the umbrella, shielding me without being asked.

"You heard the detective. You're not allowed to fly."

"Ha-ha. Very funny. I can still walk."

"You have got to be kidding, Sara. There's a killer out there! And you want to walk home in the dark? You're already soaked to the bone and you're still shivering."

When he put it like that, I had to admit he had a good point. I did not want to run into a murderer, however unlikely that might have seemed. Then again, I supposed Bree hadn't thought it was very likely either. I glanced back toward the library where her body lay. What on earth could have happened to Bree?

"Come on," said Jason. He stepped away from the ambulance and held out a hand. I took it begrudgingly because the last thing I needed now was a face-plant onto the wet tarmac. With my hand in his, he hesitated, and seemed at a loss over what to do next. I had to give him the benefit of the doubt. It wasn't everyday that a person got interviewed about a murder. Jason probably regretted his decision to pull over and see what was wrong. After a moment, he inclined his head, and guided me to his car, placing one arm around my waist. He opened the door and closed it after me. I didn't know how badly I was shivering until he climbed in behind the wheel and turned the heat on full blast. "Are you okay?" he asked as he deposited the closed umbrella into the rear footwell.

I nodded mutely.

"Really?" he pressed, looking at me more closely.

I stared back at him, unsure of how to answer. Instead I stared at the snowflakes clinging to his eyebrows. One slid down, rolling past his eyes. I didn't realize how brilliantly blue they were until then. I shook myself. Jason's eyes weren't the topic I should have been focusing on at that moment. "Just shocked and upset and... I can't believe someone would hurt Bree. She is so... she was so nice," I corrected myself, shivering again.

"I'm sorry. That was a horrible way to die." Jason started the car, sliding past the police cars just as lightning flashed in the sky, illuminating the library. The wipers were running at full speed, splashing the snow to the sides. Jason drove carefully, a little under the speed limit, and we didn't speak until he pulled up outside my house.

"How did you know where I live?" I inquired. I knew I hadn't told him and he never asked.

"Does it matter?"

"Yes!"

He shrugged. "It's a small town. I bet you know where I'm staying too."

I wanted to say I had no idea but instead, I nodded. Bree had already told me a week ago. She was picking up a couple of books the hotel employees discovered in their sitting room and she saw him eating breakfast through the big picture window. "The Maple Tree Hotel," I said. I had gone there several times. My mother took me to lunch there for my last birthday and we sat outside, beneath the famous maple trees the hotel was named after.

"I'm staying there for the duration of this trip."

"You mean, until the escrow closes on the library?" I asked, rephrasing the statement.

Jason's jaw stiffened. "A bit longer than that but yes, that's part of it. Let's not talk about it now. It's really not the best time."

I wanted to say if he were around, it was always the best time, but I also remembered my manners. He was being nice enough to drive me home while I dripped water all over his smart leather upholstery; and there was the other possibility that he might have saved me from being killed too. He was right, it wasn't the best time to argue about the library. There was always tomorrow, and every day after that until one of us won the fight.

"Thanks for the lift," I said, a little bit more stiffly than I intended.

"I'm glad you're okay," he said at the same time, our words meshing together. He started to say something else, but then stopped. He turned off the engine, his hands pausing on the steering wheel like he was still deciding if he should speak. Apparently choosing not to, he got out of the car, walked around and appeared at my door. He opened it and offered me his hand. I took it, frowning at the unexpected chivalry, and he helped me out, closing the door behind me before stepping towards the narrow path that led to my front door. Evidently, he intended to walk me the whole way.

"You really don't have to escort me," I protested but I was too cold to hesitate or stop. I just wanted to get inside. I also hoped Jason didn't expect to be invited in. I wanted to shed my wet things, run the bath, and try to banish the awful sight of Bree lying dead on the floor. Detective Logan gave me my purse but I couldn't imagine reading my book now, not after a real crime had just happened.

"I know," said Jason, continuing to walk next to me.

When we got to the door, I felt as awkward as a teenager. What was I supposed to do? Shake his hand? Invite him in for coffee and hope he said no? Offer to pay him for the gas? After a moment's hesitation, I remembered exactly why Jason Rees was in town. He intended to close the library, and nothing more. Bree's murder would probably manage to help his cause in some horrible way. He was being nice only because he had to. By tomorrow, everyone in town would have heard about the murder and collectively agree that the library should be closed for good. A leaking roof and rattling windows were one thing; murder was quite another. Plus, if he were anything less than polite to me, everyone would soon know that too. Calendar wasn't famous for its ability to stifle idle gossip.

"I appreciate the lift and thank you for looking after me," I said, opening the door with wet, shivering fingers after stabbing at the lock a couple of times. Tears stung my eyelids and a wave of fear and shock returned in a rush. I needed to be alone. "Good night," I said, my voice shaking as I shut the door before Jason could reply.

I waited on the other side of the door, cringing at my abruptness. So I wasn't exactly warm but Jason could hardly expect me to be the welcoming committee even if he were being kind. He'd already brought me enough bad news earlier, and I dreaded to think what he might return with tomorrow after imparting this latest event to his firm. So while I appreciated the lift, and his timely arrival to the library, and waiting with me while the police and the ambulance arrived, and propping me up while Detective Logan asked all of his questions, I refused to be duped into thinking he was some kind of savior.

Or handsome.

As soon as I thought it, I pulled a face and exiled the concept right out of my head. I definitely was not going anywhere with that on my mind.

Instead, I switched on the lights, walking from room to room in my small house, filling it with light and closing all the curtains. The last thing I wanted now was darkness. The dark would only remind me of Bree lying alone on the library floor, her blood pooling under her head, and her lifeless eyes staring at something no one on this earth could see.

Detective Logan's question came back to me: *What can you tell me about her?*

I filled the tea kettle with water and set it on the stove to boil while I busied myself with finding a cup and some sugar. Waiting for the water to boil, I grabbed a cookie from the jar and nibbled on it, thinking about the question that I still couldn't answer.

Bree first turned up at the library three months ago, asking about the job I posted on the notice board in the entryway. It was a job no one else applied for, leaving me to run the library almost entirely alone for over a month. Tired and desperate for any help, I interviewed Bree over a cup of coffee. She bubbled with enthusiasm about books and reading, while eagerly endorsing all the events I was planning to entice new readers and old, even throwing in a few ideas of her own. Best of all, Bree could start right away. Moving to Calendar in order to seek a new direction in her life, she said that even though she had never worked in a library before, she insisted she would love it. I was so tired and relieved that I instantly offered her the job on the spot.

We were friends ever since that day. At least, I thought we were. Having spent a lot of time together since then, I trusted her. Bree was chatty and cheerful, but now that I thought about it, perhaps that was all empty chatter. The weather, the library patrons, the latest books we read. I didn't actually know very much about her at all.

No, that isn't exactly true. I did know a few things. Bree's parents passed away when she was just a teenager and there was a brother still living somewhere. She had grown up in a large city but was it Syracuse or Salt Lake City or Seattle? I couldn't remember. She had some experience working in bookshops but never a library until I hired her. She liked reading fiction and soon borrowed a number of romances, claiming they were her secret indulgence. She wasn't very drawn to the non-fiction section but told me it was time to put it to good use. She chose to make it her special project and spent a lot of her spare time trying to make that section more interesting and appealing by creating pretty displays in the waist-high glass-topped display cabinets dotted all around the library. The local kids loved her when she put on silly voices and had no shame in prancing around and pretending to be a dinosaur or an alien during storytime.

It wasn't just the kids either. Everyone seemed to like Bree. She easily remembered their names and the books they liked, as well as previous conversations. She was always making people feel welcome.

We went out socially a few times and Bree had an easy-going way about her that prompted people to talk to her while she simply listened. She had a unique talent for listening, I suppose, that ensured Bree never really had to *say* anything. I tried to recall a single time when Bree mentioned she was going out with anyone else, be they friends or a date, but I couldn't think of any at all.

The tea kettle whistled, startling me, and I switched off the stove. I had to force myself to breath steadily and more deeply, knowing that only time could settle my nerves. Time and learning the truth of what happened to my friend.

I lifted the kettle off the stove and poured the boiling water into my cup, adding a tea bag and sugar. I let it steep while I warmed my hands on the outside. Inside, however, my tears filled my eyelids and threatened to spill over.

I couldn't stop thinking about a very important question that dominated all the other thoughts in my mind. Why would anyone want to kill Bree?

CHAPTER THREE

My mornings usually started off simply with a routine I created years ago. After getting up, I made my bed and plumped the pillows, took a shower, and dressed in the clothes I dutifully laid out the evening before. I ate quickly, standing up in my kitchen, before walking to the library. It was partly for the exercise and also because it would have taken me more time to back my car out of the driveway, drive there, and park again, than it did to walk. It was an easy, uncomplicated routine that I always enjoyed.

Over the past month, I even managed to allow myself a brief sleep-in since Bree would already have opened the library. By the time I got there, Bree would also have already switched on the lights, and the heating would have kicked in. A pot of coffee would be warming in our little side room that doubled as an office and break room. We looked after the patrons, prepared for or carried out the events on the schedule, and worked as a tag-team for lunch if it was very busy, or ate together when it was quiet. Afterwards, if necessary, I would pick up my car and run some books over to the Senior Center and performed any number of tasks that involved leaving my desk, dropping my car off at home, and returning in time for Bree to leave early.

Throughout the night, I kept worrying that Bree only stayed late yesterday to help me with storytime and I wondered if it somehow contributed to her death. Rationally, however, I knew it couldn't have. The children had all gone home and I thought Bree left too.

Today was unlike my usual routine. After drifting off into a fitful sleep in the early hours, I awoke but still felt very tired. The library was closed, surrounded by crime scene police tape when I walked past. Naturally, I was unable to resist the urge to check up on the old building. Now I was at the police station and facing Detective Logan from across his desk. He called, asking me to come in and I promptly raced down there, hoping he had some news.

"I don't understand. Why would anyone kill Bree? She was such a nice person," I said.

Detective Logan let his pen hover above his notepad. "That's what we're trying to determine, ma'am."

"Do the members of her family know?" I asked, ignoring that he called me *ma'am* like he barely knew me. Sam Logan was several years older than me, and although we never shared the same social circle, I was sure he knew what my name was. He used it only last night. I figured he was trying to be very professional, a hard challenge when you've grown up knowing everyone else in town and they you. I wondered if that small town vibe was partly why he hadn't returned for so long after finishing college.

"We were hoping you could help us with that."

"I'm sorry. I don't know them. Bree's family never came to the library, not as far as I knew and they don't live in Calendar."

"Do you know where Bree came from?"

I opened my mouth to answer before I realized I didn't know that either. It was just like a whole bunch of questions I asked myself last night. Bree never said where she came from. It was almost like she deliberately mentioned a lot of different places to confuse me. "I don't know," I said, wincing at how inadequate I sounded.

"Do you know any of the names of the people in her family?"

Aside from Mom and Dad? I wanted to ask. Instead, I simply shook my head. "Perhaps there's an address and phone number book at her apartment? I think she has a brother." I tried to recall his name but couldn't grasp one. I was sure, however, that she had mentioned a brother.

"We searched her apartment last night and didn't find anything. No names, no phone numbers, not even a home phone line."

"That's strange. Are you sure there wasn't an address book stashed somewhere?"

"We searched everywhere," Detective Logan said, sounding exasperated.

"What about her cellphone?"

"No sign of it on the body, or at her home. It's been switched off."

"Do you think the killer might have taken it?" I asked. When he said "the body," I instantly felt sick. Surely Bree wouldn't have been killed for a phone? "It was an older model, nothing fancy or expensive, just a plain, old, not-very-smart phone. Bree barely even used it. I doubt it was worth too much."

"Regardless, we have to assume the killer took it."

I wondered whom he meant by "we." Everyone in Calendar knew that Detective Logan did most of the work that was reported to the police station. His senior officer was only months away from retirement although the generally relaxed attitude began several years ago. The senior officer was more than happy to hand over the workload to Logan. Usually, there wasn't too much crime in Calendar. Logan could handle whatever came up, but every so often, he looked like he'd barely slept.

"Then you can trace it!" I exclaimed. "I know they do that on all the cop shows. It could lead you right to the killer!" Finally, a true spark of positivity rose in me, one which the detective quickly dashed. It was delivered with the same kind of patient face I reserved for the really irritating customers at the library.

"We're on it," he assured me. "I know you were in shock yesterday but I hope you had some time to think and try to remember. What else can you tell me about Bree?"

"She hadn't worked for the library very long but she was lovely. Always so nice to the customers. She was never late and she never took advantage of her lunch breaks. She was always clean and tidy..." I trailed off at seeing the detective's disappointed face. "That wasn't what you were looking for," I finished, observing his indifference to Bree's attention to punctuality.

"Do you actually know *anything* about her?" he asked.

I pulled a face. "U-h-h..."

"Like where she grew up, or went to college? Did she ever mention her high school? What was her last job?" pressed Detective Logan.

"I do know that!" Finally, there was something I did know! "She worked in a bookshop. I called them for a reference before I offered her the job. I might have their name and number at home or maybe it's at the library."

"Call me as soon as you find it," said Detective Logan. He plucked a business card from a small pile on his desk and handed it to me. His desk phone number was printed on the front. "What was the name of the business?" he asked.

"I don't recall. I know I wrote it down though, along with the phone number."

"Do you know anything else? Did she drive a car?"

I shook my head. "No."

"How did she get into town?"

"I don't know. By bus, I guess."

"We'll check," said Detective Logan without looking up. "Did Bree have any social media accounts?"

"No, she was a technophobe. She only used the library computer under extreme sufferance."

"Did you know her at all before she came to Calendar?"

"No, I didn't."

This time, Detective Logan looked up, watching me. "Any ideas why she came here? It's not exactly on most people's bucket list of places to live and work," he said, his voice sounding weary.

I smiled. That was true. Calendar was a sweet town, and popular with tourists who liked its quaintness. Although there was an abundance of brick built shops topped with pretty colored siding and signs in matching antiqued fonts, it lacked a buzzing nightlife, bars, theaters, excluding the little one created by the Amateur Dramatics Society, or anything else glamorous enough to attract a big crowd. Most tourists left after a few hours of browsing the antique shops, sporting goods stores, and cafés, or taking part in one of the seasonal activities like the Fourth of July town party, the Halloween Haunted Gardens tour or the annual Christmas parade. If there was one thing Calendar really excelled at, it was celebrating. There was usually always some kind of town event in operation. Adding to its festive appeal was the town's geography. Nestled at the base of a mountainous region, Calendar was extremely picturesque. It never failed to attract many campers and hikers from spring until fall. In the winter, skiing became the most popular pastime. Except for the tourists, the majority of people who came to Calendar only did so because they were related or friendly with someone who lived there. Rarely did a stranger blow in and stay for very long. "I know, but something must have attracted her to this town," I told him, wishing I knew what it might have been.

"I would ask if you knew what that could be, but I'm guessing the answer is no." He waited patiently for me to shake my head. "Thought as much. Listen, Sara, here's my problem. We've got a dead body in the library, discovered after closing hours. We also have a very narrow window of time for the murder to have occurred, thanks to your accurate memory of when you left and returned. I figure Bree must have let herself in, and maybe her killer too, but I don't know why. We don't know who else was in there with her and we don't have the weapon that was used, a gun. We don't know the killer's motive and we can't find out a damn thing about the dead woman! Don't you find those circumstances a little suspicious?"

"Bree was obviously a very private person," I said. A strange feeling was growing deep within me and I didn't like it. It was the same gut reaction I had when I knew my ex was cheating, and also when I discovered my college roommate was reading my papers and using my research to write her own. The unpleasant, sticky feeling that something is wrong also crept up on me a few minutes before I found Bree's body. I just didn't know then what might have caused it.

Detective Logan continued talking, "A dead woman, whom no one seems to know anything about, and has no past, or anything that ties her to something or someone, is very worrying."

"Do you think she was trying to escape from something?" I asked. I read a book like that once. The beautiful, young woman fled from an abusive husband and started her new life with an assumed identity. She thought she was safe until he came after her, heralding a renewed reign of terror. The protagonist devised all kinds of things to give herself a fictional past when she arrived in a town she had no connection to. A town where she hoped she would never be found. "Like maybe from a husband or boyfriend? Someone she was really scared of?" I asked.

The detective gave me a long, silent look that made my fingers fidget in my lap. "I appreciate you coming down to the station," he said finally.

I wondered why he didn't answer my question but decided Sam Logan was not in a very friendly mood. Mostly, he looked weary and exasperated so I figured my lack of answers was a major contributor to his ennui. That, and I assumed he didn't relish the thought of breaking Bree's death to her family when he eventually managed to find them.

"When can I reopen the library?" I asked since I couldn't think of any other questions. Detective Logan failed to tell me anything about Bree's death beyond what I already knew; and he didn't seem any closer to apprehending the culprit. I wasn't really that eager to get inside, not so much as being worried that the library might never reopen. Bree wouldn't have wanted that. She was every bit as determined as I was that the library should remain open. Jason Rees hadn't stopped by with any more bad news, not since yesterday, but it was only a matter of time before his firm persuaded the town council to abruptly closed the library's doors for good. Corpse or not, I had to get inside and start working on my rescue plan. I needed something positive to focus on and to keep my head from filling up with terrible thoughts.

"We should be done with our investigation in a couple of days."

"A couple of days!" I exclaimed, my visible disappointment upsetting me.

Detective Logan's brows knitted together. "Are you that eager to clean up?"

"What? No!" I cringed at the idea of cleaning up my friend's spilt blood. It didn't occur to me last night that there could have been some blood left on the library's wooden floor, probably all dried up and sticky now. I would have to search online for the best way to remove it, or even better, ask someone from the town council to hire a professional cleaning service. Scratch that. They probably would only complain about the budget and say no, adding that to the list of reasons why the library should be torn down.

I wasn't sure I wanted to do the cleanup, or even if I were that keen to reopen the doors again. Thinking that Bree perished there while I walked around like nothing had happened was a horrible thought. Yet if I didn't reopen it, Jason Rees would, no doubt, seize the opportunity to knock down the library at once, without any opposition from me. That made my decision easy. "Please tell me when I can reopen the library," I told the detective. "I'd like to open it up again as soon as possible."

"Sure will. You know, however, that a lot of people will just want to come in and take a ghoulish look at the crime scene?" Detective Logan warned.

I shuddered. "Then I'll insist that they sign the petition to save the library before I let them in," I said.

"What are you going to do until then?" Detective Logan asked. He dropped the pen on his notepad and rocked back in his chair, visible curiosity filling his eyes. At least, I hoped it was curiosity and not suspicion.

"I intend to find out something important about Bree," I replied, almost regretting the words as soon as I said them. I grabbed my purse as I stood up and slid the detective's business card into the small inside pocket. I couldn't stop myself from blurting out, "I feel terrible that I can't even answer your simplest questions; and I also want to know why she never told me anything personal about herself."

"Don't you start anything like an investigation," warned Detective Logan. "I advise you to stay away from this nasty business. I hate to say it, because I don't want to scare you, but you were very lucky last night. We could easily have driven two bodies to the morgue."

"I was just lucky Jason turned up when he did," I said.

"Yeah? Lucky timing," said Detective Logan. This time, I concluded he did look suspicious, but was it because of Jason? "This is nothing like your mystery novels. This is real life and there's a real murderer out there."

"You're right, this isn't like any mystery novel," I told him, hoping he assumed I was just agreeing with him. But as I left, I thought, *It really isn't. This is real life and I'm not going to let someone get away with murder!*

CHAPTER FOUR

I looked at the chocolate sprinkle-covered cupcake in front of me and wondered if it were a comfort offering or possibly a bribe. The three pairs of eyes watching me convinced me that it must have been a little bit of both. The eyes watched me pick it up and take a bite, which I slowly chewed.

"It's just so unbelievably awful," said Jaclyn Henry. She owned the Coffee Corner, a smart, little café situated on Calendar's main square. She was currently off work, owing to a broken leg she sustained over the new year. Fortunately, her assistant, Candice, took over the daily management, but that didn't stop Jaclyn from stopping by to check on it every couple of days.

"A murder in Calendar! We don't even have burglaries," added my mother. She untied a colorful scarf and draped it over the back of her chair, along with her amply padded, down coat. After running into her on Main Street, only a few minutes walk from the police station, I was not surprised to find out that she already knew about Bree's murder. She insisted on taking me to the café for a treat. I figured by treat, she meant an interrogation and since I had the time, I allowed her to guide me inside. My mother looked a lot like me with dark brown hair and brown eyes. My hair, however, was swept up into a ponytail, and highlighted with caramel streaks, while hers was a pixie crop. She had a terrific sense of style that I could only hope to emulate.

"Finding Bree must have been terrible, Sara. She was always so sweet." The last comment came from Candice, the one who placed the cupcake temptingly in front of me. Jaclyn insisted that it and the marshmallow-and-whipped cream-topped hot chocolate were "on the house."

"Do the police know who might have done it?" asked Mom.

I looked at their expectant faces and decided they wouldn't be disappointed by the lack of progress. "I spoke with Detective Logan this morning and I don't think so. It has only been a few hours," I reminded them.

My companions collaborated in a mixture of soothing and shocked noises. I was pretty sure I heard someone mutter that "grouchy" Detective Logan needed to work it out quickly and smart. I held back a smile as I bit into the cupcake again, savoring the chocolate icing when it dissolved on my tongue. In another life, I could have happily trained as a chocolate taster.

"He needs to find a girlfriend," said my mother. "Doesn't that man ever date?"

I stifled a laugh, reminding myself of what we were really talking about: Bree. Dating women was the least of Sam Logan's worries. The detective had earned a reputation for not being the happiest of souls although no one really knew why. The hottest rumor was because he suffered a tragic heartbreak sometime in his past. That morsel was usually followed by the assertion that he really needed a new girlfriend. Or maybe a boyfriend. No one really cared so long as someone could cheer him up.

Jaclyn reached for my hand. "Thank goodness Jason Rees got there and found you. You could have been killed too!"

"He's very handsome, isn't he?" said Candice, barely holding back a giggle as her cheeks flushed pink.

"He is not!" I told them and my mother's eyebrows rose at my quick denial of Jason's good looks. "He's trying to close the library down so he can build tract homes."

"The bastard," said Candice, her eyes narrowing comically. "How dare he provide homes for new families while also saving our friend? Let's run him out of town!"

I couldn't help laughing at her mock indignation. "He didn't save me," I told them. "He just happened to drive past the library and saw the door was open. I guess he thought someone had broken into the library. He heard me scream before he got me outside and called the police. Then he waited with me until the ambulance arrived. That's all," I told them, surgically excising some of the bits like when he wrapped his arms around me and held my hand far longer than necessary. I thought about adding that he was probably hoping to find some graffiti or other traces of vandalism but decided that was just being mean. I truly had no idea what he could possibly have ever hoped for.

"That's so manly," gushed Jaclyn. She leaned into the table, cupping her chin in her palm and eagerly waiting for the next thing I had to say, which wasn't much.

"Anyone would have done the same thing," I said, shrugging as I tried to think of someone else.

"Not in Calendar! We have a severe shortage of heroes," said my mother. "Jason Rees was very brave. He had no idea what he was running into, and let's not forget that he did save you, darling."

"He's not a hero!" I didn't know why I began protesting so vehemently. Apparently, my companions thought Jason really was a hero. My mother was even getting a little misty-eyed. This was not good. If Jason managed to gain a glowing reputation, my campaign would have been ruined before I even started.

"Poor Bree though," said Candice. "What a terrible way to die. I can't imagine why anyone would want to kill her."

"Neither can I." I sighed, remembering last night's questions and this morning's interview. "It's strange, but only after Detective Logan started interviewing me did I realize I didn't know much about Bree at all."

"I know she came from Salt Lake City," said Mom.

"No, Nadine, she was from Seattle," corrected Candice.

"It was definitely Salt Lake. She had a sister," said Jaclyn.

"No, she had a brother," I corrected her, then stopped. When everyone else remained silent, I added, "She said she previously worked in a bookshop."

"It was a clothes shop."

"I heard she was a personal assistant," said Mom.

"We obviously know nothing about her," I told their puzzled faces.

"Sure we do. She, uh, ah... Hmmm." Candice stopped and grimaced.

"I think she was on the run," I told them. Collectively, they leaned in. "She turned up in Calendar right out of the blue and nobody knows where she came from. She didn't tell anyone of us the same story and no one can verify anything she did tell us. I think she was on the run, maybe from a man," I posited as they exhaled shocked gasps.

"No way!"

"Makes perfect sense."

"Poor Bree!"

"Maybe her ex found her and killed her. Do you think he might have been stalking her?" asked Candice. She briefly checked the door for customers, then gave up the pretense of hovering or looking ready to serve, and pulled out the chair next to Jaclyn.

"She never mentioned she thought someone was watching her," I said, thinking back hard. No, Bree appeared perfectly normal. She never seemed worried either, but that didn't mean she wasn't secretly. But now that I thought about it, she was somewhat distracted all week. I assumed it was her concern over the library closing and potentially losing her job, even though it wasn't ever threatened. Now I wondered if there could have been another cause. "It also doesn't explain why she went back to the library after we closed," I finished. I thought about divulging what Detective Logan said about letting her killer into the library, but decided not to. That could have been official police information and I didn't want to add more fodder to the gossip train. I'd already inadvertently told them enough.

"Maybe she left something?" said Mom. "Could that be why she went back?"

"Like what? She had her purse when she left."

"A book?" asked Candice.

"She already had two checked out. I suppose I'd better collect them from her apartment. I have her spare key."

"Maybe you could take a little look around while you're there?" suggested Jaclyn.

The table fell silent as we each thought about that. "I don't suppose it could hurt," I decided. "Someone needs to locate her family and tell them. Detective Logan said he already searched her apartment but maybe he missed something."

"You mean there's no one to bury her?" Mom's jaw dropped in horror.

"No one that I know about. Oh!" I smiled as I remembered something I hadn't thought to mention to Detective Logan. "She filled out a form for her next of kin. All the town council employees do it. I have it in my office at the library, along with her reference." My shoulders slumped. There was a big problem with that. "Detective Logan says I can't go in."

"You should tell him though. It might be important," said Mom.

"I should," I agreed. I took the last bite of the cupcake, enjoying the rich chocolate. I didn't have many vices but chocolate consumption was definitely at the top of the list. Also, in second and third place. "I'll call him soon and tell him where to find that information. I better go. Thanks so much for the cupcake, Jaclyn."

"Don't thank me," protested Jaclyn, holding her hands up. "Candice is the baker. I am very lucky to have her."

"Thanks, Candice."

"My pleasure. Anything I can do, just let me know. We all liked Bree," Candice added to a chorus of agreement. "And it's horrible to think an ex-boyfriend might have stalked and killed her."

I grabbed my jacket from the back of the chair and slipped it on, zipping it up. The snowstorm had ceased sometime in the night, leaving a broad expanse of blue, cloudless sky in its wake. The snow was already melting. Every lawn had perked up, glistening green, but it was still bitterly cold. I added my hat and gloves before slinging my purse across my shoulders. I said goodbye to my mother and promised not to go anywhere dark, or alone, and no, she didn't need to invite Jason to dinner as a thank you, or even send him a card. I wasn't sure what etiquette dictated at times like these but I believed I could handle a genuine thank you by myself.

Detective Logan told me I couldn't go to the library but he hadn't said anything about entering Bree's apartment. With little else to do on my strictly enforced day off, I decided that would be my next stop. Then, I could go home and try to figure out how to contact a member of Bree's family after I provided the information to the police. The thought of her lying cold and alone inside the morgue haunted me and I shuddered. I knew her family would welcome a friendly, helping hand once they arrived in Calendar. Knowing that none of her loved ones, if any existed, even knew where she currently was made me feel awful. If she were in hiding, they might not even have known where to look for her. They couldn't have known she was dead. It made more sense to give Detective Logan the necessary time to contact them before I stepped in and offered my friendly, local help. It was the least I could do for Bree.

I paused with my hand on the door handle. It seemed a little crass to ask, given the news I'd just shared with my friends but I had to. "You're all planning to support my campaign to save the library, aren't you?" I asked.

"Absolutely. You can count on us," chimed the chorus of replies I hoped for.

"You should make some posters and plaster them all around town," suggested Candice. "I can help, if you like?"

"Yes, please!" I replied, giving my mother and friends a little wave before I left them to continue their conversation about the case. I could hardly imagine they wouldn't. Murder was a terrible thing; and in a gossipy town like Calendar, I had no doubt it would be the biggest news for weeks to come.

I tried to think about Bree as I walked to her apartment but I was still struggling for answers. Bree entrusted me with a key to her apartment in case of emergencies since I was the only person she knew in town. She asked me to take it, only a few days after the front door banged shut behind her one day, locking her out and requiring an emergency call to the 24-hour locksmith. At first, I was surprised but also a tiny bit pleased that she considered me trustworthy. I promised I would keep the key in a sealed envelope and forget about it unless she mentioned it. I did manage to forget about it but now I knew exactly where to find it.

Instead of walking directly to Bree's apartment, I took a detour past my house and picked up the still-sealed envelope. A few minutes later, with the winter chill becoming more evident and the temperature rapidly plummeting, I parked my car outside on Oak Street. After unlocking the door to her apartment, I stepped inside. Heat welcomed me and I guessed it was still set on a timer, probably switching off while she was at work. I pushed the door closed behind me.

The apartment seemed unnaturally still, but it could have just been me. I was prone to ascribing a feeling to things that didn't really exist. But there was an undeniable echo of Bree's death that I felt strongly. Everything looked the same from the last time I visited, only a couple of weeks before. I dropped in briefly to leave her some groceries after she went home early, her red eyes and runny nose the telltale signs of the beginnings of a cold. I bought her some chicken soup from the deli, a crusty loaf of bread that was perfect for tearing off chunks to dip, two large boxes of tissues, and some OTC medicine. Two days later, Bree was back at work, apologizing more than once for leaving me to work alone.

Bree told me her apartment was furnished and now I looked more closely at the simple furnishings I barely noticed in prior visits. A couch was covered in a thin cream blanket. A coffee table with deep scratches at the corners and legs had obviously been moved one too many times and survived more than a few tenants. A remote control and a magazine were left on top of it, as if Bree would come back any moment and pick them up.

A cheap lamp and a small, flatscreen TV were the only electrical items. I moved past the TV and looked over at the mantel. Two framed photos featured a nice-looking couple in their fifties. Bree told me they were her parents. I studied them, wondering where they were now. The background didn't provide any clues. One seemed to have been taken at a party, and I saw balloons and a metallic banner in the background. The other had a pretty cabin in the backdrop, nestled beneath snow-capped mountains. A vacation home, maybe? I put the photo frames back in their places and looked around for the books Bree had checked out. It took me a few seconds to conclude they weren't in the sparse living room.

A small kitchen occupied a quarter of the living room. A cheap coffee pot and toaster sat on the counter. The single plate, bowl, and flatware on the drainer were dry. I opened the cabinet doors, looking for a slip of paper or anything else that might tell me where Bree's family lived.

Closing the last cabinet, I knew my search was futile. The cabinets, like the living room, were empty with only the absolute basics for daily living. Nothing was expensive, and almost everything was disposable. Unlike me, Bree didn't use any of her shelf space to hide her bills or correspondence or even an address book. I turned around, growing more puzzled.

In the bedroom, I found the books I was looking for on the nightstand. A sliver of paper was folded and used as a bookmark, which she discarded beside them. I assumed Bree finished reading them. I hoped she enjoyed them. I doubted I would have been very happy having a pulp romance for my last ever item of reading. As soon as that thought crossed my mind, I winced. What a horrible thing to imagine! With a sigh and a grimace, I tucked the books into my purse, fully determined not to remember their titles. Something about that made me squeamish. I didn't want to be reminded of it when the next person checked them out.

The nightstand drawer was empty, barring a hairbrush and some of the cloth headbands Bree occasionally wore. I pushed the drawer shut and moved over to the closet. One rail held an assortment of clothes, all familiar items I'd seen Bree wear. A few shoes were arranged neatly on the floor, along with a large, empty bag. The shelves held folded sweaters, t-shirts, underwear, and socks. Rifling through the clothes made me grimace but I pushed the items apart, looking for anything that might have slipped between them, something that might have had a phone number or an address. Nothing!

I stepped back and pushed the closet doors shut.

There was one place left for me to look. My search of the bathroom took all of one minute, the amount of time it took to open the mirrored cabinet and examine Bree's meager collection of shampoo, conditioner, deodorant, and toothpaste. No medicines marked with her name or even a pharmacy.

I stepped back into the bedroom and paused. I wasn't surprised that Bree didn't have an address book. I only had one because my mother gave me one for Christmas ten years ago. It was an old-fashioned thing to have nowadays. Most people put their contacts into their smartphones now. Perhaps Bree did the same. I remembered that her phone was missing and Detective Logan couldn't find it. I wondered if he'd taken the necessary steps to track it down yet.

What puzzled me the most as I looked around the bedroom was the glaring absence of anything personal except for the two photographs in the main living area. There weren't any favorite trinkets or collectibles. No birthday cards or letters or anything that had obviously been a gift. No high school yearbook or college pennants for nostalgia. No cozy pillows or pretty glassware to make the apartment more like a home.

It seemed like Bree had no intention of ever settling into her apartment. It looked more like a motel room. She could have easily thrown her clothes into a bag and taken off within an hour, maybe even thirty minutes, and fled to a new town without a backwards glance. I recalled a book I once read where the protagonist victim managed to pack all of her things in a "go bag" so she could get out of wherever she was in less than thirty minutes. If her husband were close by, she had to move as fast as she could to avoid being found by him.

I paused in my search, thinking about the things I would take with me if I needed a fast getaway. If I were on the run, I would need much more than just my clothes. I would need my ID too. If Bree had anything like that, it wasn't visible. I tried to think like a woman on the run. Someone who was scared of her own shadow. I would definitely hide it, I decided, just in case anyone discovered my address and got into my apartment. Any further away, and the documents would have been too hard to get if I needed to leave in a hurry, like say, in the middle of the night.

Starting in the living room, I began running my hands down the sides of the sofa, then under the coffee table. I opened the oven and the slim dishwasher, peering inside, and used my fingers to feel around the gap between the top and the counter. I stood on tiptoes to see the top shelf of the cabinets. Nothing. I pulled myself onto my knees on the counter and stretched upwards, peeking at the gap between the cabinets and the ceiling. Nothing but dust.

In the bedroom, I checked under the bed and in between the mattress and the divan base. The fabric was ripped and threadbare with age but nothing had dropped down to the floor. I patted each shelf in the closet and stepped over to the nightstand, pulling open the drawer and feeling underneath.

My fingers brushed over a paper and tape.

Dropping to my knees, I craned my neck down to see. An envelope was taped underneath the drawer. I peeled off the tape and pulled the envelope free before pushing the drawer shut.

When the apartment door suddenly opened, I froze.

"I'll check everywhere," said a male voice I didn't recognize. "She wasn't that smart. She must have hidden it somewhere and I'm not leaving town without it."

CHAPTER FIVE

My hiding place was dark and cramped. I held my breath, my heart thumping with fear, and waited for movement, unsure of how long I was curled up tightly at the base of the bed. The footsteps finally exited the room and the shuffling of bedclothes along with the opening of drawers and closets stopped too, but I couldn't tell how long it had been. I guessed ten minutes but without any light to check my watch, I couldn't say for sure. I was too afraid of turning my cellphone on in case the light seeped through a crack in the base that I hadn't seen, thereby revealing me to the mystery man. Counting slowly seemed to help until I began to stumble over my numbers.

Now I listened intently for any sound but couldn't hear a thing. The last big noise I heard was what I hoped was the front door opening and then shutting but I didn't really know about that either.

There was only one thing I was sure of: I couldn't stay hidden in the bed frame forever. If the man came back with the intent of tossing the place, I didn't want to be there for him to discover. Whatever he was looking for, it definitely wasn't a person. He was looking for something Bree must have hidden; and his assertion that "she wasn't that smart" meant he thought that whatever she hid had to be here.

With shaking hands, I pushed the mattress up and listened carefully. When I couldn't hear anything but the sound of my own breathing, I hoisted myself out of the ripped frame, tumbling onto the floor like a newborn lamb. I waited breathlessly, but no one came. He must have left.

I didn't know exactly what made me hide the moment I heard his voice but I was so glad I did. Concealed inside the bed frame, I heard him stomping through the apartment, cursing as he searched in vain. I tried not to think of what could have happened if he knew I was there. He might have threatened me or much worse.

What if he were the man who killed Bree?

Leaning back under the mattress, I pulled out my purse and slipped it across my shoulder. Creeping forward, I peeked out from the bedroom door. Everything looked the same. The man hadn't trashed the apartment. He must have been careful not to disturb anything; or else he put it back the way he found it. If I hadn't already arrived at Bree's apartment first, and let myself in with her spare key, I would never have known someone else had searched her home. I figured that must have been his plan.

Hurrying to the windows at the front of the apartment, I peeked out, checking the surrounding area for any traces of the man. No one loitered on the street and all the cars I could see were empty.

There was only one way out. Bree's door led into a common corridor where three other apartments opened onto. Taking a deep breath, I slowly opened the door and slipped out, pulling it closed behind me, and waiting for the click to indicate it was locked. If the man still lingered somewhere outside, I could only hope he thought I exited from one of the neighboring apartments. Before I left, I turned, stooping down to look at the lock. The tiniest of scratches were evident around the keyhole. I didn't know if they were there previously but I felt sure he must've picked the lock! Whoever he was, Bree never intended for him to have access to her home.

Jogging down the stairs, I hurried to my car and beeped it open. I was careful to check the backseat just in case someone lurked there in wait for me, and I hit the locks as soon as I climbed inside.

The incident really scared me. Who was the man and what was he searching for? He obviously thought Bree had hidden something, which he didn't think would be hard to find. Yet, I was sure he left empty-handed because the only thing hidden in the apartment was the envelope which now lay inside my purse. That definitely purposefully concealed, since it was so securely taped to the underside of a nightstand drawer. Whatever it was, Bree didn't want it found.

Igniting the engine, I forced myself to drive, even though my hands were still shaking. I couldn't stop shaking until I got home. The journey took me three times as long as it should have because I chose an unusually long route. I wanted to see if I were being followed but fortunately, I wasn't.

Inside my house, I locked the door and checked the handle before flopping into my armchair and trying to calm down. Nothing happened. He hadn't found me. I wasn't hurt.

Where did that thought come from?

I realized it arose at the same moment I heard his voice. He was, as my mother would say, *up to no good*. I had to tell Detective Logan. Could this be the man who hurt Bree?

Detective Logan gave me his card. I pulled it from my purse and held it up while I dialed his number.

"Detective Logan," he said when he answered.

"Hi, it's me, er Sara. Sara Cutler," I stammered.

"Are you okay?"

"Yes, thank you, yes, I am." I stopped and took a deep breath. "Actually, no. I went to Bree's apartment and a man came in there."

"Who?"

"I don't know. He came into the apartment and I heard him say he was looking for something."

"Did he say what it was specifically?" asked Detective Logan, his voice belying his sudden interest.

"No; just that she must have hidden something and he intended to check everywhere. I couldn't hear another voice so he must have been talking on the phone to someone."

"Can you give me a description?"

"Of the phone?"

"The man," sighed Detective Logan.

"Oh, yes, of course. That is, well, actually, no." I winced, feeling small and stupid. "I heard him and I hid," I admitted, wishing I could crawl into a hole and disappear. I called the detective with a lead but had no real information to give him. "I was inside the apartment and I became too afraid."

"Your friend was murdered. You were right to be cautious," said Detective Logan, his voice softer and more sympathetic. "Now may I ask, what were you doing in Bree's apartment?"

"I thought I'd see if anything needed to be done, like, uh, watering the plants," I told him, scrambling for an answer that didn't involve searching for clues. I was pretty sure Logan would bristle at the idea of me butting into police business.

"I see," he said without sounding convinced. "Tell me what happened, starting from when the man first came in."

I explained what I heard and added, "I stayed hidden in the bed frame until he was gone."

"Do you know if he found anything?"

"I don't know for certain but it didn't sound like it. I didn't hear him say 'Aha!' or anything like that and he didn't make another call either."

"But he didn't say what he was looking for?"

"No, but whatever it was, he thought Bree had it. Do you think it could be the same man who killed her?"

"Could be, or someone connected to that person, or to her in some way. I'll admit it sounds pretty suspicious." Detective Logan paused and I waited for another question. Instead he said, "I'll look into it. Please don't go into the apartment again. If he's searching for something that he thinks Bree had, it could be the motive for her murder. I don't want you painting a big, fat bull's eye on your back."

"I won't," I promised. "Did you locate any of Bree's relatives?"

"Not yet." Detective Logan hung up after giving me another warning not to go back to the apartment. I promised I wouldn't and meant it. His idea that I might become the next target wasn't unreasonable. Whatever was missing must have been something important to someone. And if this man were the actual murderer, then I was sure he wouldn't hesitate to add another body to his list.

Only after I dropped the phone onto the coffee table did I remember the envelope. I pulled it from my purse and turned it over, looking for any indication of what it might contain, or even an instruction of *when* to open it. Both sides, however, were blank. I squeezed it, finding something bulky and rectangular inside and turned it over. I began frowning as I noticed the opening was taped shut. The ends of the tape from where I peeled it from the drawer still hung from each side. I knew I should have called Detective Logan again and probably handed over the envelope but I couldn't resist taking a look inside. I pulled at the flap and opened it, deciding I would see the contents first and tell Logan later. Bree was my friend, after all, not his. For Logan, it was business; for me, it was personal.

I shook the envelope's contents into my hand, my eyes widening when I saw the edges of a passport. I pulled it out and a driver's license popped out too, along with a wad of money.

The license photo was of Bree but the name on it said Brittany Johnson not Bree Shaw. The registered address was in the state, but not at her Oak Street apartment. The passport had the same name and Bree's photo. I put both of them aside and counted the money. Three thousand dollars in twenty-dollar bills!

Why did Bree need so much money? Why had she hidden it? And why did her passport and license identify her as Brittany Johnson?

My mind circled back to the theory I first hit upon in the café. If Bree were on the run from a man, it made sense for her to change her name so that it would be harder for anyone to find her. Bree could easily be shortened to Brittany. Perhaps the surname she'd given to me was her maiden name? No, whoever she was fleeing from would know that name. She must have given me a fake one. Perhaps the passport was her married name? Having never seen a fake passport before, I just assumed it was genuine but maybe it was a fake too?

For whatever reasons, Bree felt it necessary to keep these documents hidden. The money, I could understand. It was enough to buy her a plane or train ticket, maybe even hire a car to cross state lines. Or she could have been intending to use it as a deposit on another apartment or a few nights in cheap motels. It had to be her running away money.

The man in the apartment must have been her ex.

No, that didn't make sense. If he tracked her down and killed her, why wouldn't he have already left Calendar or tried to put as much distance as he could between the crime and himself? What could have been so important that he would have chosen to stick around and find it? Had he killed her in a previous attempt to get it?

Although I thought about it a lot, I still couldn't work out why Bree would have returned to the library. Maybe the mystery ex found her so she'd taken him there rather than returning to her apartment. Perhaps she thought he would calm down and she could possibly call for help?

Without realizing it, I'd gotten onto my feet, and begun pacing the living room as the unanswered questions swirled in my head. I wished I was a PI, like Kathleen Turner in *V.I. Warshawski* on TV or Sam Spade from the mystery novels. Then I might have known what to do and how to go about finding out what happened to Bree. Detective Logan would know what to do though.

I looked down at the envelope in my hand and I knew I had to give it to him. It wouldn't be right to withhold information, especially if it could help solve the crime. But could it also change the focus of the investigation and direct it elsewhere? What if he jumped to the conclusion that Bree had done something wrong?

Before I handed over any evidence, I had to make a copy.

After placing the license on my coffee table, I took out my phone camera and snapped a picture. I checked to be sure it was clearly visible and I could read all the words and subsequently repeated the action with the passport, which I wedged open at the photo page. I also took a photo of the stack of money.

When a knock sounded at my door, I jumped. I didn't realize how jangled my nerves were until that moment and I could only laugh at my own fright. As I crossed the room to the door, I tensed up. What if Detective Logan were right? Could the same man have followed me here? What if he'd been watching me through the window? He'd know I had the envelope! I quickly retraced my steps, stuffing everything back as I'd found it and depositing it in my purse.

More knocking came. I was all alone. My closest neighbors were probably at work.

I softened my footsteps as I approached the door and took my phone in hand, ready to dial 911. Before pulling the door open, I checked the peephole, and gratefully exhaled a sigh of relief.

Jason Rees was outside on my stoop.

I thought about tiptoeing away but decided to get it over with. Whatever Jason wanted, I don't know why he couldn't have gone to my boss.

"Hi, Sara," he said with a smile. Glancing over his shoulder, as if suddenly he regretted knocking and was trying to spot his getaway car parked at the curb, he said, "I hope you don't mind but I was thinking about you."

I blinked back my surprise. "You were *thinking* about me?"

"I was worried about you… after yesterday. I came to check on you earlier but you were gone."

"I had to go down to the police station. Detective Logan wanted to talk to me."

Jason nodded knowingly. "I just came from there. Detective Logan looks like a man with a lot on his mind."

"I don't think he ever expected to have to solve a murder case in Calendar."

"He's a detective!"

"And this is Calendar," I pointed out as Jason's frown lifted. "We're so safe here, it's positively boring."

"That's one of the reasons my firm was drawn to this town. Families love to feel safe and they need safe homes." Jason stopped and took a breath. "Sorry, I didn't come here to talk business. I just came to check on you. Last night must have been unbearable for you. I can't imagine how you must feel today..."

"It was. Thanks for checking on me; but as you can see, I'm fine."

"You received a horrible shock," he said, his voice gentler.

"Yes, I did," I admitted, "but I have to keep on... I don't know." I threw my hands in the air as I struggled for the right word. Finally, I settled on, *living*. "I have to keep living."

"I was worried that you might fall apart."

I wondered if Jason expected to find a sobbing heap when he saw me. He would get more than a surprise if I told him what I'd really been doing! "I'm not that kind of person," I replied, sucking in a deep breath and pushing my shoulders back. It was making me braver than I felt. "Plus, it would have been pretty awful if I started to wail and cry every five minutes. Bree was my friend but I only knew her for a few months. There must be plenty of other people who will be devastated at hearing about her untimely death and I don't want to overstep my boundaries. Besides, I'm much better off staying calm and helping wherever I can."

Jason gave me an impressed look. "You're the kind of person people need in an emergency. Level-headed, smart."

Ha! He thinks I'm smart. I pushed the thought away as my heart thumped irregularly, feeling quite pleased now. "Like I said, Calendar is generally safer than safe. There aren't a lot of critical emergencies happening here."

"Do you want to take a walk with me? I know you're not at work because of what happened and I already saw the crime scene tape all around the library."

It was my turn to frown. "A walk?"

"You know..." Jason mimed putting one leg in front of the other, swinging his arms in clown-like movements. I bit the insides of my cheeks to stop my laugh from emerging. "How about showing me the town?" he suggested. "I think we have a clear window of no snow and the rain the weather report promised isn't here yet. We should be okay for the rest of the morning."

"Okay," I agreed, my eager acceptance popping out of my mouth unexpectedly. I needed to go past the police station anyway. Besides, I wasn't sure how I could politely shake Jason off. Perhaps a pleasant hour spent showing him the finer points of Calendar would convince him that I was fine and didn't need to be looked after. Even better, maybe I could show him another location for his housing development! One that didn't involve tearing the library down. "Let's go."

CHAPTER SIX

Calendar attracted plenty of tourists, both local and from afar, for a good reason. The quaint mixture of brick buildings, clad with prettily-colored siding and little shops topped with signposts in matching antiqued fonts, imbued it with a quintessential beauty that made people feel instantly at home. Most of the visitors became nostalgic for simpler times and many were determined to become a part of such a cozy community. Even if it were only for a day.

I wondered how Jason felt about my town now that the cozy aspect to it had been marred by murder. Would his firm still want to build new homes on the same site where a woman was killed?

"Have you lived here all your life?" he inquired, surprising me by asking such a personal question. After a few comments about the town, we walked from my house on Maple View and headed south towards Main Street. He admired the contrasting array of attractive homes while I imparted a few town facts, and we passed the last few minutes in silence.

I shook my head, thinking back to the first day I laid eyes on the town. "Not quite. My parents moved here when I was just five. My dad was the principal of the high school and my mom had a teaching job. They always wanted to get away from the city and live in a nice, safe place where they could raise a family."

"You never wanted to go back to the city?"

I shook my head. "I thought about it a few times when I was in college. It was great studying in the city. All the parties and bars and the usual buzz, but it never felt right to me. I guess I've always been a small-town girl at heart."

"You don't look like a small-town girl."

I paused, glancing at him as I stopped. "Why? Because I'm not wearing dungarees or chewing on a piece of straw?"

As if I just slapped him, Jason stopped, and began looking down. "No, I meant, I... I don't know what I meant. You seem very smart and educated and passionate."

"You get all sorts here."

"I didn't mean it as an insult." Jason ran a hand over his hair and blew out a breath. "I bet you think I'm just some jerk of a city guy."

I studied him, wondering if I did think that. The first time I saw him, I actually thought he was gorgeous, but he quickly ruined that when he informed me of the library's imminent sale. He was still gorgeous, but I managed to ignore that every time I saw him after that. Sort of.

"Aren't you?" I asked.

"No," came his blunt reply.

I started again, hastening my pace but Jason caught up quickly, and his long stride easily outpaced mine. "So, you don't drive an SUV even though you live in the city, which is hardly rugged terrain, and you don't have a penthouse apartment with a skyline view?" I paused, seeing Jason wince as my unsympathetic guess hit a chord. Finally, I'd struck a nerve. "Thought so," I told him. Yet, I didn't feel smug; I felt rude.

"I'm not as bad as all that."

"I bet your watch cost more than I can earn in two months," I told him. "And I'm pretty sure any of your suits must exceed a thousand dollars."

"Two actually," said Jason. "And the watch was a graduation gift from my parents."

"You aren't the first wealthy man to stroll into Calendar just to make some money at the expense of our town." He probably wouldn't be the last either. However, he was the first one who made any attempt to talk to me like a person.

"I'm trying to provide appealing family homes, and I'm not looking to make a quick buck."

"And all you need to do that is to first bulldoze our historic library."

"No, but we need to move the library regardless. It's in an old building with a leaky roof and the windows are dropping from their frames. I plan to provide the town with a new building for the library and a lot more inside space. The vacant land will be put to excellent use."

"Glad you've got it all figured out." My phone rang in my purse, stopping Jason from his next unbearably sensible retort. "Excuse me," I said as I answered.

"Sara?"

"Yes, it's me."

"It's Marta," said my boss. "Why didn't you call me last night? Where are you?"

I winced. "You heard?"

"I did. It's awful, just awful. Poor Bree. You must know the library is closed still."

"Yes, Detective Logan told me."

"You should take a few days off. I insist upon it. What a terrible shock for you. What are you doing now?"

"Just taking a walk. Is everything okay?"

"As much as it can be right now. I just spoke to Detective Logan and he said the library can't be opened until tomorrow, or the day after. Apparently, they finished all the necessary processing, or whatever they call it. I can find someone to fill in for you if you need to take a few days off," said Marta, and her voice was oozing with genuine compassion.

"That's good news, Marta, but I don't need any time off. I'd rather work. Did Detective Logan say if they found anything?"

"He wouldn't say. It's very worrying. Do you know why Bree was there so late? Detective Logan said you had both left for the day."

"I don't know. She shouldn't have been there. She had already gone home when I locked up. I only went back when I realized I forgot my purse."

"Well, thank goodness you weren't hurt too! Listen, Sara, it might be a good idea if you collected all your personal things as soon as you can," said Marta.

"Why?"

"I'm going to meet with the council later. Even though Detective Logan says he'll have the library cleared for re-occupancy very soon, I'm not sure we'll reopen it. It's too horrible to think about. Not only what happened there but the upcoming sale..."

"But it isn't sold yet!"

"I'm afraid this is the final nail in the coffin," said Marta. "I know you don't like it but the council were very disturbed with this recent... *you know*. I have to go to a meeting now, Sara, but we'll talk again soon. Stop by the office when you can and we'll talk about undertaking the library's relocation." Marta hung up and I dropped my phone into my purse.

"Are you okay?" asked Jason.

"Fine," I said, feeling anything but. I was furious. Furious that Bree was dead and that the council would dare to use her death as another reason to close the library! I didn't even get a chance to put my plan to save it into action yet. Walking around with Jason had instantly become the last thing I wanted to be doing. "Actually, do you mind if we continue this tour another time? I have to do something right away."

"No problem."

After directing Jason to Main Street, which was now only minutes away, I left him. Moving quickly before I started to apologize to him for leaving him in the lurch, I knew that he meant well by checking on me. But that didn't mean I had to spend my unscheduled spare time by entertaining him. So what if he had down time too?! That didn't surprise me. A murder in the library must have surprised Jason's whole firm. The echo of Marta's glum comment still rang in my head, and I knew that it couldn't have adversely affected him. All it could possibly do was speed up the whole process and ensure the library would be torn down.

I frowned, remembering something else. Marta said I could go in there and collect my personal things. I decided to do exactly that, except instead of getting my items, I would retrieve the contact details Bree left there. Once I had those, I would go to Detective Logan and take him the package I found. Having frantically thrown it in my purse when Jason came to my door, it began to weigh a little too heavily on me. I did not like to carry around that kind of money.

Turning the corner, I tugged on my gloves and aimed for the library.

The crime scene tape I expected to see still fluttering across the door had been removed. The only thing slightly abnormal now was that the lights were all turned off. For once, there wasn't a steady trail of people coming and going through the main doors either. I figured word of the crime must have flown very quickly. I pulled my key from my pocket and before I could lose my nerve, I unlocked the door. As I stepped inside, my heart began to thump loudly.

The library was quiet and cold, making the stillness more than oppressive. I flicked the lights on, one after the other until the old building was fully illuminated. I couldn't move.

From my spot inside the door, my hand was still resting on the handle as I looked around, searching for anything out of the ordinary. It struck me that I'd never been frightened in here before; but now, all I felt was fear. *Was that how Bree felt?* Did she realize her attacker was also in the building? Or did he surprise her? Did she even know he was there? Or had she invited him inside for some unfathomable reason? Had he subsequently betrayed her trust?

If Bree didn't know, how could I?

"No one is going around randomly killing librarians," I said aloud, settling on what I believed to be true. Someone wanted something from Bree, not from me. I stepped forwards and behind me, the door whipped shut, slamming into its frame. I whirled around, my heart thudding harder, but no one was there. Exhaling a relieved breath, I turned around. I had to pull myself together. Bree was killed because of something, or someone, she was running away from. I had nothing to worry about from my past that could haunt me now. I didn't have to be afraid. All I had to do was walk across the floor and let myself into the small office on the other side.

Sucking in a breath, I pushed back my shoulders, and strode forward, crossing the floor faster than I ever did before. I worked the key chain, moving from the big door key to the smaller, newer office key. I pushed it into the lock, turned it, then pushed the door open. I propped it against the wall using a large door-stopper. The kids from the local high school made it for the library a few years ago. I considered nudging the door-stopper out of the way and closing the door against any intruders, but later decided it would be worse to open the door again without seeing what was out there first.

The room smelled of yesterday's coffee and the air was quite chilly since a small draft leaked through the window that overlooked the garden. Moving around the desk, I searched through the drawers, seeking the file that contained Bree's personal information. When I took over managing the library, I made a point of clearing out all the old paperwork, and sending several boxes to be archived. The only personal information left was that belonging to me, Bree and a couple of people who worked part time hours. Bree's folder was on top. I pulled it out and opened it. She listed a bookstore in the city as her only reference.

Grabbing the office phone, I dialed the number. The line was dead. I replaced the handset then picked it up and tried again. Still no active dial tone.

"That's weird," I said, double-checking the dates she listed. Bree wrote down she last worked there only four months ago. I called the operator and asked for the store, reeling off the address.

"There's no store listing by that name, ma'am," said the audibly bored operator.

"Are you sure? Can you check...?"

"I'm sure," she drawled.

"What about anything similar to that name?"

"There's nothing similar. Can I help you with anything else?"

"No, thank you," I said and hung up. Instead of powering up the library computer, I reached for my cellphone and opened a browser window. I typed in the store name. No search results.

I typed it again, adding the address Bree wrote down. Still nothing.

I thought for a moment, then an idea popped into my head. I opened up my maps app and typed in the address, prompting a view of the street. I swiped my finger until the address matched the one Bree gave. There was no bookstore, only a series of business addresses and small store fronts punctuated with chain restaurants.

An awful, puzzling thought entered my head. Bree deliberately gave me a false address. Yet, I was sure I verified the number when I checked the reference and I knew I had spoken to someone. With my worry rising, I concluded that Bree must have made the whole thing up just so she could get the job.

I turned the page, looking for her next of kin, information that the council insisted all employees fill out. Mine had my mother listed. I was pretty sure the only time they would have to look it up to make a call would be if someone had a heart attack, or got electrocuted by the old wiring. I was absolutely certain that they never anticipated a murder.

Bree wrote down the name of her parents, listing an address in the city, and a phone number. I dialed it, certain that it would it dead too, but instead, the phone rang and a woman answered.

"Hello, is this Mrs. Shaw?" I asked, checking the name Bree gave me.

"No, this is the Whedon residence," she said. "This is Clara Whedon."

"Does a Mrs. Shaw also live there?"

"No, she doesn't."

"Has she ever in the past? Maybe she moved recently? Or have you just been assigned this phone number?"

"We have have lived here for eleven years and the phone number hasn't changed!" she said, sounding slightly irritated.

"Do you know someone called Bree?"

"No," she said, her patience rapidly vanishing.

"Brittany?" I tried next, already knowing what her answer would be. "Maybe a Mrs. Johnson?" I added, remembering the license with a different name.

"I don't know what scam you're trying to..."

"This is the number?" I asked, reeling off the number I just dialed.

"That's correct."

"Sorry to disturb you. I must have gotten it wrong then," I said, realizing this was one more fruitless call.

Strike two I thought as I hung up, staring at the worthless pieces of paper. "Who are you, Bree?" I asked the empty room. "Is everything you've ever told me a lie?" I sighed, knowing that the answers could not be found here. The best thing to do now was to see Detective Logan and hand over Bree's passport and license in another name. I also had to tell him about the false information.

I closed the drawers and tucked the file into my purse before shutting the office door behind me, and locking it. I hurried across the floor, only pausing briefly at the staircase. I didn't want to go upstairs but something compelled me. What was Bree doing up there? Before I could change my mind, I jogged up the stairs and stepped around the balustrade, walking over to where I found Bree's lifeless body.

The body was gone now, of course, and the only thing left to show for the murder was a dark stain on the parqueted floor. I didn't have to get closer to it to know it was blood. *Bree's blood.*

I stared at it for a long moment until I looked away, gulping down my unease before I started to cry. I forced myself to focus on what I could see. There wasn't a lot in this section. Bree decided that the area needed refreshing and she scoured the basement for new props to use. She intended to make the first display about astronomy. Between the two of us, we carried an old display case from the basement up to the second floor where Bree carefully cleaned it. Adding jet black paper for a backdrop, she created an impressive montage of planets and stars with glittery crystals she found in the sewing shop. She added old astronomy books and compiled a guide to the books people should read for more information about the universe. It was both clever and charming.

A month ago, she suggested a pirate display. Starting with a small old chest from a thrift store, she painted it to look like a treasure chest and stuffed it full with strings of colorful, glass beads. She also pressed clay into the shapes of old coins and painted them gold, scattering them around the chest with brilliant glitter and paste gems. She included several pirate books, and again, added her own personal guide. I had to admit it was genius, and the patrons truly loved it, but looking at it now just made me sad.

Glancing away, I made a fast walk to the entrance, turning every light off and locking the doors. The sadness filled my heart. How could anyone snuff out Bree's fun, creative spirit?

On the way to the police station, I rehearsed what I would say to Detective Logan. He would probably be cross that I'd already checked Bree's personal information and found it false; but I supposed he couldn't really complain since he would have gotten the same result. He might even be pleased with the packet I gave him, so long as I glossed over how I managed to get it. It was probably best he didn't know. He had a reputation for being a grouch and I didn't want to tempt him into arresting me, especially after he'd warned me off Bree's apartment.

The police station didn't look busy when I arrived at the front desk. "Is Detective Logan here?" I asked.

"Sure, he's in his office," started the young officer, looking up from the Sudoku puzzle he was studying intently. "What's it regarding?"

"It's about Bree," I told him.

"Bree?"

"The same woman that was just found dead in my library," I explained, exasperated. *Which Bree did he think I meant?* "I'm Sara Cutler. I found her."

"Ohhh," he said, nodding now and his eyes started lighting up. "Let me call... Nope, here he is... Detective?" he said just as Detective Logan strode around the corner. "Sara Cutler's here..."

"Not now," yelled Logan.

"It's important..." I started to argue, but he cut me off and yelled an instruction to his colleague. "I'm heading over to the paper to chew them out over this," he said, waving the newspaper in his hand.

"But I have something very important..."

"It can wait!"

I started after him when he jogged outside. "It's about Bree. I found something you should... Excuse me!" I said, bumping into a man and ricocheting off him in my haste to keep up with Logan.

"Leave it with Joe," Detective Logan yelled over his shoulder. Heading for his police cruiser, he rudely shut the door on me, leaving me sputtering and alone just as a downpour of rain began to fall.

CHAPTER SEVEN

I couldn't stay there, standing on the street, watching Detective Logan disappear behind a veil of rain. So I pulled up my hood and stalked away in the direction of Main Street. I decided to treat myself to a hot cup of coffee and wait out the rain before I went home.

Ramming my hands into my pockets, I tucked my chin beneath my scarf and hurried towards the café, cursing Detective Logan under my breath. I couldn't imagine what could have been more important than hearing new information about Bree! *Unless*, I pondered, *he just received some new information of his own?*

I briefly considered turning around and going back to the station. I could try to wheedle the information out of the young officer I guessed was Joe but as I glanced that direction, I decided against it. It would almost certainly be futile, plus, Joe might insist on knowing what information I had. The only hands I dared to leave that information in belonged to Detective Logan.

"You look mad," said Candice as I stormed into the café after the bell above the door announced my entrance. My mother and Jaclyn left and no one else was sitting at the tables Candice had just finished cleaning. "Soaked, too."

"Will this rain ever stop?" I muttered dejectedly, looking down at the little puddle I created on the café floor. The downpour was heavy and already washing away the snow.

"Sure, around March," Candice laughed. "Come on in before we need a mop. Let me take your jacket and scarf and I'll put them close to the heater. Do you want me to take your purse too?"

I thought about what my purse contained and shook my head. "Please, can I have the biggest cup of coffee you make? I'm so cold."

"Your hands are nearly blue!" Candice said.

I looked down at my hands before patting my pockets. I extracted one glove, and my shoulders dropped in disappointment. "I must have lost the other one," I groaned as the bell chimed again. Candice took the jacket and held it out, dripping. She moved to the wall rack and gingerly hung it above the heater to dry.

"Like this one?" said a voice behind me. Turning around, I saw a tall man with dark blonde hair holding out a glove. He smiled warmly.

"Where did you find it?" I grinned as I took it from him. My precious leather gloves were a luxury purchase I made a couple of years ago. Finding one of my pockets empty as I walked into the café was just another disappointment of late.

"I saw you drop it outside the police station. I called after you but evidently, you didn't hear." He smiled warmly, and little crinkles appeared around his eyes.

"I must apologize." I winced. I must have been so utterly absorbed in my own thoughts that I failed to hear someone calling aftcr me. "You followed me all the way here?"

"When you put it like that..." The stranger pulled a face as if I intended to accuse him of stalking me. "I hope you don't mind but it looked like such a nice glove and I figured who would want to lose a nice glove on a day like this?" He nodded to the rain that poured incessantly outside.

"Me!" I agreed, a huge wave of gratitude washing over me. "Thank you so much! Could I buy you a cup of coffee as a way of properly thanking you?"

"Oh, I..." He checked over his shoulder.

"You're waiting for someone," I guessed. "I am so sorry for making you follow me all the way over here. Thank you so much for picking up my glove."

"No, no, it's not that! I just thought, that's the nicest offer I've had all day! Thank you! I'd love a cup."

I couldn't help smiling at him and then at Candice who gave me a quick thumbs up behind his back. "I'm Sara," I told him, reaching out my icy-cold hand to shake his.

"Tom," he said, grasping my hand with his warmer, gloved one.

"Pleased to meet you."

He smiled and said, "The pleasure's mine."

"You two take a seat and I will bring your coffees to you," Candice said, beaming. "I just took out a batch of brownies from the oven. It's a new recipe too. You have to try it! I refuse to hear a no. You two can be my guinea pigs."

"Guess we're sampling the brownies," said Tom, his smile growing broader. "My day just keeps getting better and better."

"Surely it can't be that bad! Not that coffee and brownies couldn't fix it?" I asked.

"Throw in the company of a pretty lady and I think I can say my day has been saved."

I indicated the table in the window, heartened at the unexpected compliment, and we walked over. Tom slid out my chair as attentively as a waiter in a fancy restaurant and I sat down. He took the seat opposite, placing his back to the wall. "I just drove a very long way to get here and the hotel lost my booking. I'm not sure where I'm going to stay tonight. Any tips from a local?"

"Actually, yes, I can give you the names of a couple of bed-and-breakfasts, if that will help?"

"That sounds perfect!"

"What brings you to a town like Calendar?" I asked, finding him quite pleasant and approachable as I assessed him. Tall, and good looking, with dark blonde hair curling behind his ears almost to his collar, and a clean-shaven jaw. The little crinkles around his eyes put him in his thirties. He shrugged off his gloves and jacket. I saw a black sweater with a blue shirt collar underneath and added, "You don't look like one of our typical tourists."

"You get tourists even in winter?" he asked, looking out the window as if he didn't believe me. "I have to say, I preferred the snow to this rain."

"We sure do get winter tourists. Calendar is big on all kinds of events so there's usually something happening here every month."

"Really? What's happening this month?"

"Actually, maybe I made this town sound more interesting than it really is. With the new year celebrations gone, the only events in January are those at the library." My shoulders slumped as I realized what I said. That probably wouldn't be happening anymore now though. "I need to backtrack again. The library is currently closed," I explained as Tom waited patiently.

"How come?" he asked.

I paused, suddenly suspicious that Tom might have been one of Jason's developer colleagues. However, he didn't seem at all familiar with the library. "There was a murder," I explained.

Tom's jaw dropped open but he recovered quickly. "That's terrible! Did they catch the killer?"

"Not yet."

Tom leaned back when Candice placed our coffees on the table along with a plate of brownies. She sprinkled a dusting of powdered sugar across the top, using a doily for a stencil.

"Wow. I thought I was coming to *Cutesville*, certainly not the newest murder capital."

"You're not! This is Calendar's first murder in I don't know how many years. I swear," I said, placing my hand over my heart.

"Were you and the victim close?"

I nodded glumly. I didn't want to explain that I once thought Bree and I were friends, because now I wasn't sure. That was too much information for a stranger. "We worked together," I said. "I'm the head librarian."

Sympathy shone on his sincere face. "I am so sorry. I didn't mean to pry. This has to be awfully horrible for you."

"It is," I admitted, "but it's probably so much worse for her family."

"They must be very upset," Tom said.

I shook my head. "I don't know if the police managed to track them down yet. Bree was a very private person and a relatively recent resident."

"Well, I hope they turn up," he said, "and I hope someone is looking after you too. I think the general advice in situations like this is to keep busy."

"I wish I could! With the library now closed, I don't know what to do," I told him. I wasn't ready to add just what I'd been doing to keep busy. I couldn't be sure what the kind stranger would think about my private activities. He would probably wonder if I were crazy. *First, I spent my morning searching Bree's apartment and hiding in her bed frame; then I continued my investigation into her past by calling her fake references!* If someone told me that, I would advise them to tell the police and let them solve it, but somehow, I couldn't take my own advice. It had become too personal.

"If that's the case, maybe I can help?"

"Do you have a library that needs cataloguing?" I asked with a smile.

"Not quite. I have my digital tablet but it's pretty organized as well as being compact. I was thinking that maybe I could take you to dinner. What do you say?"

What did Bree always like to tell me? She kept advising me to live a little! Suddenly, her recommendation meant more to me now than ever before. "That would be really nice."

"Why don't I pick you up tomorrow at eight? Oh, wait! I don't know your address and I guess you could consider me a stranger," he said, laughing. "Why don't I meet you somewhere? I saw a pretty, little French restaurant across the street, the one with some huge trees outside the door? Francine's?"

"I can meet you there at eight," I agreed. I'd been wanting to try the restaurant since it changed menu for the new year but never got the opportunity. A date with Tom seemed like the perfect chance. Plus, Tom was right: it would take my mind off other things. If I stayed home, all I would end up doing would be to worry myself silly.

"That's great! I have to run right now because I have an appointment; but I'm really glad I ran into you, Sara." Tom smiled warmly as he got to his feet and held out his hand. I took it, puzzled momentarily when he raised it, but he leaned down and kissed my knuckles with soft, cool lips. "Until tomorrow night."

"That was so romantic," squealed Candice. She slid into Tom's seat the moment he disappeared from view. "Who was he? Where did you find him?"

"His name is Tom and he found me. He saw me drop my glove and he followed me all the way here."

"So chivalrous!" Candice sighed.

"He also asked me out on a date!" I tried to repress my pleased smile but I couldn't help letting some of it break through.

Candice's eyes widened. "That is so amazing!"

"I know!"

"Where are you going? What will you wear?" she asked, her excitement crowding her questions into fast succession.

I told her Tom had already picked the restaurant. "I don't know what to wear. Do you know how long it's been since I went on a date?"

"Too long, I'm sure," said Candice. "I have no idea why you don't date more often. Don't you realize how pretty you are? And don't try to brush me off! This calls for a new dress."

"No!" I shook my head, thinking of the unnecessary expense but also feeling a little silly. I wasn't the kind of woman who rushed out for a new outfit on a whim. I could probably wear something I already had.

"I mean it! You need a new dress. I bet you can't remember the last time you bought a new dress either. You've been through a horrible couple of days and you should treat yourself."

"Do you really think so?"

"No, Sara, I *know* so," said Candice with absolute certainty. "I know what happened to Bree was terrible; but I now give you all the permission you need to live your life to the very best it can be, starting with this date!"

I left the café, warmed not only from the hot coffee, but also the unexpected encounter, and my good friend's determined advice. The sun finally emerged, bright but cold, barely peeking through the clouds to signal the rain was over. I decided I would take Candice's advice and with my free time currently abundant go over to the small boutique on the other side of the square. She was right about my clothing options; I had a few dresses in my closet but none of them were particularly suitable for a first date. Most were left over from Calendar's long, warm summers, and I had a couple of smart woolen suits for winter wear at the library. Going out attire was largely limited to a few smart blouses that I usually wore with jeans. Yet, the more I thought about the forthcoming date, the more I knew I wanted to impress Tom. Although he was only wearing a sweater and slacks, he had an air of refined elegance about him.

"Hi," called Meredith Blake, the boutique's owner, waving to me as I stepped inside the shop. "Sara! It's so nice to see you!"

"Hi," I greeted her warmly when she came over to give me a welcoming hug. I hadn't known Meredith for too long – she'd only opened the boutique a year ago— but she was always gracious and friendly whenever I saw her.

"This isn't a social call, is it?" asked Meredith. "I already signed your petition to keep the library open."

"I know, and thank you for that. No, I actually came here for a new dress."

"Really? What kind of dress were you thinking of?" Meredith studied me, searching for an answer that didn't involve *work* or a *funeral.* That thought made me feel awful. I didn't need a new funeral dress because I had a simple, black wrap dress that would work just fine. No, I needed some cheering up. Since I couldn't proceed any further with solving Bree's murder, I was determined to take Candice's advice. I gave myself permission to enjoy life.

"For a date," I told her shyly, waiting for the inevitable excitement.

"Well, it's about time!" gushed Meredith. She laughed and flicked her blonde hair over her shoulder. "Do you know how long I've waited for you to come in and ask for a cute, dating dress? Sacha, come and help me!" she called out and a teenaged girl with long, brown hair and big, brown eyes walked through the door from the rear of the boutique. "This is my new Saturday girl, Sacha. I'm training her today," explained Meredith.

"Hi, Sacha."

"Hi, Ms. Cutler," Sacha said, smiling prettily.

"When was the last time you bought a new dress for a date?" asked Meredith.

"Um, never?" I had to guess. Glancing down at the knee-length, dark, knit dress I currently wore with long, flat boots, I immediately felt drab against Meredith's chic wrap dress and sexy heels. Even Sacha was stylish in a trendy, teen sort of way. Wearing a lacy, white top and slim, black pants along with a dramatic, silver bangle, Sacha seemed quite fashionable.

" Let's see. You have a great figure and that gorgeous, chocolate-and-caramel hair... I bet I have a bunch of dresses that you would look great in! Since it's winter, I suppose you'll want to wear stockings, so maybe we should look for a dress with a heavier weight to the fabric, like this green dress?" Meredith reached for a hanger from the rack behind me and held it out. The dress was made from thick satin and featured a neckline slashed unbearably low.

"I can't wear that on a first date!"

Meredith's face fell. "Why not?"

"It's really beautiful but I'd be so afraid of falling out of it," I said, waving a hand over the front. "It's rather revealing."

"You are more of a demure girl," agreed Meredith, nodding as she replaced the dress and reached for another hanger. I had to stifle a laugh at being called a girl; Meredith had to be in her late twenties, the same as me! "What about this cute, black number? Sacha, can you check the sizes we have in stock? Hmm, no, it's a little too drab, looks like it's for someone who died, not... oh, I'm sorry!" Meredith clapped a hand over her mouth. "That was such a stupid slip. I can't believe I said that when your friend just died."

"You heard?"

"Honey, I think everyone heard. I just can't believe it. I only spoke to Bree last week when I picked up one of those thrillers I love to read. Poor girl. Did they arrest whoever did it?"

I shook my head. "Not yet. They have no suspects yet."

"I wonder if it had anything to do with that phone call I overheard," she said as she rifled through the rack. Assessing and discarding several dresses in quick succession, she continued firing instructions to Sacha to check for a dress she thought she had in the back.

"What phone call?" I asked when the teen hurried away.

"It was last week when I came in and borrowed the book. Bree's cellphone rang and she stepped out to take it. I wasn't listening, I promise, but I overheard something..." She stepped back with another dress in hand and presented it to me. I wavered my hand, conveying my uncertainty toward the busy, floral print. More interesting was what Meredith had to say. "What did you hear?" I asked.

"I wouldn't repeat this if she were still alive but it sounded like she was having an argument. She kept saying that she was never coming back. And she also said to stop looking for her. She sounded very frustrated and a little bit angry."

"That doesn't sound like an argument. More like she was warning someone off."

"Yeah, that wasn't the weird bit though. She kept saying she was in Florida."

"Florida?"

"Yeah, not exactly within throwing distance of Calendar, huh? I figured she wanted the person on the other end to think that she was somewhere far away from here. Isn't it strange?"

"Very," I agreed, recalling my original theory about Bree running away from a boyfriend. "Do you think she was speaking to a man?"

"I don't know. She could have been. I wasn't trying to listen in. I was just waiting inside the library door for the snow to stop beating down so I could run out to my car and the door was open a little. Do you think I should tell someone?"

"Yes," I decided. "I think Detective Logan should know about it. I don't think he's at the police station now, but I'm sure he'll be back there today."

"Okay, I'll call him later in case it's useful information. Let's find you that dress." Meredith clapped her hands together and gasped. "I think you should try on a bunch of different styles," she decided when Sacha returned, holding up a long gown. Meredith shook her head immediately. "Too formal. I know. I have some that are perfect but you should try on a few different ones. You never know when you're going to try something on that you'd never normally pick out to wear and find it's perfect. You have plenty of time, right?"

I thought about the closed library and Detective Logan tearing out of the station. Since I'd normally have been at work at this time of day, and my usual schedule had been upset on short notice, I didn't have anywhere else to go. Before I could answer, I thought about something Bree told me only days ago. I could be anyone I wanted to be. What better way to do that than by starting with a brand new dress? "Yes," I told Meredith, instantly making my mind up. "I have plenty of time."

Meredith handed me dress after dress, insisting that I try on shoes and purses with each one, while Sacha hurried around the store to collect and replace the various items. I hated to think how much trouble I was causing them but they both seemed to be enjoying themselves. Meredith exclaimed her approval for some dresses and shook her head at others. She handed over all kinds of belts, and took them away, turning up hems and cinching in waists until finally, she had nothing left to say.

"What?" I asked, a rush of panic filling me. "Is it that bad?"

"No!" Meredith took me by the shoulders and turned me around so I could see my reflection in the full-length mirror. The dark blue sheath had a sweetheart neckline, and a translucent fabric rose from it and across my shoulders to meet with the back. The fabric draped from one side, accentuating my waist and falling to just above my knee. With the addition of black hose and lacy heels, I looked great! No, actually I looked better than great and I felt fantastic. I almost reached out to touch the mirror and be sure it was me. "It's perfect!" I said, staring at my thrilling reflection.

"You look great, Ms. Cutler," said Sacha, giving me the thumbs up.

"Doesn't she? I knew it but I'm glad you tried on all those other dresses. You needed to shake up your style a little bit, Sara. You are lucky that you can wear so many styles."

"I don't have a lot of occasions to, however," I admitted.

"Maybe you will if this date becomes a second date and a third! We sell lingerie too," she added with a wink.

I blushed. "I'll take the dress."

"Let me know when you've changed and I'll wrap it up," said Meredith. She slid the curtain shut and I heard her footsteps retreating amid the sound of rustling fabric. By the time I stepped out of the changing room, I felt much better about myself. My life might have taken a downturn in some ways but at least, I still had one. As the new year progressed, I kept thinking about all the changes I needed to make. Perhaps now was the time to do it. Bree's death was a horrible shock and I wasn't sure I could ever make sense of it; but I learned one thing: I couldn't go back to being boring Sara Cutler. I couldn't be someone who only lived for work. Not anymore. I wanted to feel alive. This dress was a tiny step towards it; the date an even bigger step. If the date didn't work out, at least I would have gotten a beautiful, new dress even if it was expensive.

"You're in luck!" squealed Meredith. "It's the last one! I just checked the tag and this dress is forty percent off during our January sale."

"Seriously?" I gasped. *Baby steps,* I reminded myself, *and maybe a smile from the universe.*

"Yes. I'm really pleased you're the one buying it." Meredith showed Sacha how to ring the dress up at the register while I put my card into the machine. Meredith promptly wrapped it in tissue before slipping it into a bag and adding a pink ribbon around the cord handles. "I was just thinking," she said, hesitating. "Oh, it's nothing. I'm probably being silly."

"What? Is it about the dress?" I wondered if she'd made a mistake and was too embarrassed to say.

"No, no. It's about Bree. I was thinking about that conversation I overheard and I just remembered something else. I heard her say that all she had to do was *lay low* for a few more weeks before she would be on the beach without a care in the world. It just struck me as a really strange comment. What do you make of it?"

"I don't know," I said honestly, "But I'd sure like to find out."

CHAPTER EIGHT

Stepping onto the sidewalk, my fingers wrapped tightly around the cord handles, Meredith's final words kept echoing in my mind. "Laying low" didn't sound like something a woman on the run from an abusive ex would say. It seemed more like something a person would say if they had something very valuable to hide.

I thought back to the envelope inside my purse. It seemed to grow heavier the longer it remained inside. I wanted to march over to the police station and thrust it into Detective Logan's hands but he'd torn out of there so fast, I couldn't be sure he'd even returned yet. I glanced in the direction of the police station and sighed. The envelope would have to wait.

First, I wanted to go home and hang up my new dress so it didn't get all wrinkled. Then I wanted to look more deeply into Bree's past. So many things didn't add up. First, her name as I knew her, and the name in the identity documents that didn't correspond. Then there were the gaping holes in her background and each of my friends having a different version of the story. It couldn't have been possible for everyone to have heard it wrong. That left only one logical explanation: Bree must have told everyone a different background history.

That didn't make any sense to me. Wouldn't it have been a lot smarter to stick to one fake story? Or perhaps she never thought it would matter. If Meredith overheard her phone call correctly, Bree never planned to stick around long enough to care.

I turned away from the direction of the police station and walked along the empty sidewalk, huddling into my coat, pulling my scarf up to my chin, and thinking about Bree's clashing stories. I believed her completely when she told me anything about herself. It never even once occurred to me that she might not have been telling the truth. Why should it? I'd already offered her the job; and she had nothing to gain by lying to me.

I thought again about what Meredith said. Would Bree have made up another lie before leaving town? Perhaps she would say she was moving to be nearer her parents or because she had another job or maybe she just planned to travel. She could have left and said nothing at all, but simply disappeared as fast as she arrived. Knowing that she valued our friendship so little she felt compelled to tell me only lies hurt me deeply when I thought about it. If she were in any kind of trouble, I would have helped her without question.

Another thought struck me. If she weren't in trouble, but actually were the trouble, would I still have helped her? I wasn't sure of the answer to that. Perhaps Bree wasn't sure either.

I stopped and waved to Grace in the New Treasures gift shop. She was working on a new display of pretty trinkets and small housewares in the window. I always admired her displays, which she changed every couple of weeks. She liked her window dressing to reflect the seasons or display any whimsical ideas she had. Last week was all about new beginnings, a change from the month-long, red and gold Christmas theme beginning in December. This week featured items that were silvery blue and had lots of mirrors. I stepped closer to take a look. It was my mother's birthday soon and Grace always had something to suit any occasion. I glanced over the photo frames and the pretty, little jewelry boxes along with some gift packs of candles and cashmere socks. My mother would like the socks and candle gift box, I decided, so I straightened up to go to the door and step inside. Just as my hand connected with the door handle, I stopped and stepped back, re-examining the selection of photo frames.

The couple smiling in the photos seemed strangely familiar. I stepped closer, stooping to look more intently. *Yes! They were Bree's parents!*

"Hey, Sara," said Grace when I stepped inside. She looked up from the box she was unpacking, and polystyrene peanuts spilled onto the French dressing table she used as a desk. "I haven't seen you since your mom's Christmas party. I was just thinking about you when you walked past the shop. I heard what happened at the library to your assistant. It's so ghastly."

"It really is," I agreed.

Grace set the box aside. "Do the police know what happened yet? Someone said it was murder but that can't be, surely not?"

I gave Grace a sympathetic nod and her eyes widened. "The police said Bree was shot," I told her solemnly.

Grace clapped a hand to her mouth. "Oh, poor Bree! How tragic. You hear of things like that happening in the city but never here. Plus, it's not like there's anything to steal at the library!"

"Not unless you want to try your luck with that big, old grandfather clock."

"I don't think that would be at the top of any thief's list," said Grace. "With the situation so fresh still, I guess that means the library is closed indefinitely?"

"Only for a couple of days," I said more confidently than I felt. "I'll open it up pretty soon. We won't close it permanently without a fight."

"That's great news! I've been meaning to come in and browse through some of your books on antiques. I've been to the estate sales, seeking a few special items, as well as some others I want to sell and it would be great to know exactly what I'm looking at beyond the pretty and sparkly. Anyway, what can I help you with?"

"I wanted to buy a gift for my mother but I saw that photo frame in the window and I wondered if you knew the people whose photograph was in it?"

"The people?" Grace frowned. "I don't put anyone's photograph inside the frames. Which one did you mean?"

I turned around, craning my head over toward the window display. "It's that one, I think," I said pointing to the large frame amid several smaller ones.

Grace reached over and plucked the photo frame from the display. "These are new. They just came in this week. This one?" she asked, holding it up and turning it to face me.

"Yes!" I pointed to the smiling couple. "That's the one. Who are they?"

Grace turned the photo frame around and frowned. "No one special. Just some stock model picture that the manufacturer puts inside the frames."

"Really?" I took the frame from her and studied it. I was sure it was definitely the same photo I'd seen on Bree's mantel several times, the one she claimed was of her parents. "I'm so silly," I said, recovering quickly before Grace thought I was acting strange. "I thought I recognized them. *Of course,* it's a stock photo. I should have known."

"The frames come from the factory with the sample pictures inside all the time," said Grace. "I thought I saw my nephew in one just last week. The little boy looked exactly like him. Were you looking for a new frame for your mom?"

"No, but I think I'll take it anyway," I said. I was sure Detective Logan would want to see it, and felt uncomfortable asking Grace for the insert. "I'll put in a new photo for my mother and get the socks and candle gift package too."

"Busy shopping day?" Grace nodded at my shopping bag when she reached for the gift box and took both of my impromptu purchases to the register.

I followed her, replying, "It wasn't intentional, but I have a date tomorrow night so I bought a new dress and while walking past here, I saw your new display, so I decided to buy my mother's birthday present too."

"Your mother will love these. I know she always likes our scented candles. I'll gift wrap them both for you."

I thanked Grace and paid her, taking the bag and waving as I left the store. Another piece of the puzzle fell into place. Unfortunately, the puzzle seemed to be growing bigger. I should have realized that photo was provided by the factory, and therefore, available for purchase by anyone. Bree must have bought the frames and simply left the stock photo inside. It appeared as though she had two parents to anyone who might have inquired about her family. I had to admit it was a good cover. I swallowed it, hook, line and sinker. I wondered if Detective Logan assumed they were her family too when he searched her apartment. If I hadn't walked past the gift shop and happened to notice, I would still have erroneously believed they were Bree's real parents.

Disappointment filled me as I embarked on the journey back to my house. Bree really did lie to me about everything. Was it because she was so ashamed of her past or because she didn't trust me? Did she trust anyone?

By the time I reached home, I was no closer to an answer. I hung my dress in the bedroom, admiring it again, and smiling when I thought about Tom. At least I still had a date to look forward to, despite my fruitless search into Bree's past.

Grabbing my laptop, I took it over to the kitchen table and opened it. While it powered up, I reached for the gift shop bag. Grace wrapped my mother's birthday gift beautifully but I pushed it to the side. Pulling out the flatter package, I tore off the gift wrap to reveal the photo frame. Opening the stand at the back, I set it in front of me on the counter and stared at it.

Why would Bree make up fake parents? Was her past life so awful that she had to invent parents? Or were they just another lie she could tell in case anyone asked? Anyone, like me.

My laptop finally came to life. I navigated the mouse icon to the browser and clicked on it before I clicked on the search bar. I typed in Bree Shaw and waited for the results to appear in a long list. There were plenty of girls with that name but as I diligently clicked on each link, none of them were the Bree I knew. I searched through ten pages until the names were becoming less exact and I gave up.

Next, I typed in her name along with the name of the bookshop that she gave me as a reference. Nothing came back in my search.

I drummed my fingers on the counter, trying to decide my next keyword. Minutes later, I typed her name along with all the cities she ever mentioned. Not one of the returned results was Bree.

Opening my cellphone, I brought up the photo I'd taken of Bree's driving license. Perhaps I would have better success with her other name. I copied Brittany Johnson into the search bar and clicked enter.

A new set of results appeared and I repeated the process of clicking each link before I ended the search. But I was no better off than I had been an hour earlier.

Perhaps I was being foolish in thinking I could investigate Bree's background. Detective Logan probably had a dozen or more programs he could search, including her fingerprints. He probably already knew Bree's back story was suspicious. Maybe he even knew her true identity.

I checked my copy of her license as Brittany Johnson. I wondered if that were another alias!

Regardless of all the lies she told, I couldn't shake the feeling that no matter what Bree said to me, we were friends. I was sure I'd spent more time with Bree than anyone else in town. We worked together and socialized occasionally. I brought her groceries when she was sick. She was the first one who encouraged me to start the petition to save the library. We made each other's coffee and shared all the tasks around the library. We joked with each other often and commiserated over the drudges and high-fived our successes. That couldn't all have been an act! I really liked Bree. Even though now I was finding out she was a different person—a *very different person*—I still liked her. No matter what she might have done, she didn't deserve to die in such a horrible and heartless way.

I had to keep looking. Not just because Bree was my friend but because I wasn't sure anyone else would look for her. She had to have a family living somewhere, and friends, people who must have loved and missed her, but where were they? And why was she hiding here under an assumed name? I gulped. Perhaps she didn't have anyone! Perhaps that was why she made up her happy, loving parents. Sadness filled me. I gulped a stoic, deep breath and pushed that thought to one side.

When neither of her names produced any useful information, I turned to the address on the driver's license. I entered it into the search bar and waited until the map turned up. I clicked on it and looked at the busy street. It was densely populated with rundown buildings and shabby-looking apartments above. The distance was estimated a two-hour drive. I checked my watch. Even if I left now, it would take too long to go there and back today. I still had tomorrow off. I could drive to the address and at least see who lived there. Perhaps Bree had a family member or a roommate who hadn't moved yet. Someone who could possibly give me some information. At the very least, I could let them know she was dead.

I turned back to the license, studying it. Having searched all the written information, I still hadn't entered a search for the photo yet. I zoomed in on the photo of Bree and took a screen capture, which I emailed to myself. Opening the email on my laptop, I copied the photo into the browser before clicking search.

Dozens of images began to fill the screen. I scrolled through all of them carefully, dismissing each one until I stopped. A grainy image of a young woman looked very similar to Bree. Her hair was longer, but she had the same pointed chin and full lips. I clicked on it, making the image larger. It was Bree! I was sure of it. I scrolled down to read the caption and gasped.

When my cellphone rang, I jumped, almost dashing it onto the floor. I thought about ignoring it as I stared at the screen but the Calendar PD number kept blinking on the screen, which made me pause. This was definitely the right time to talk to Detective Logan.

"Sara?" said Detective Logan when I answered.

"Yes, it's me. I need to talk to you right away."

"I need to speak with you too," he said at the same time.

"It's about Bree," we both chorused.

"You first," said Logan.

"I found something at her apartment and I was searching online when I saw a photo of her with an article attached. I think she's wanted by the police!"

"Yeah," sighed Detective Logan. "That's exactly what I want to talk to you about."

CHAPTER NINE

It took all of ten minutes for Detective Logan to drive from the police station to my house. By the time he arrived, I'd already paced the length of the house several times and was waiting as eagerly as the family dog at the door.

"Thanks for seeing me," he said, stepping inside and wiping his feet on the mat.

"I'm glad you called. I don't know what to make of Bree being wanted by the police?"

"Me neither but it doesn't look good. You said you ran an image search?"

I nodded. "That's right. The more I find out about Bree, the less I know! I decided to do an image search online."

"That's smart thinking."

I paused, wondering. "Is that what you did?" I asked.

Detective Logan nodded. "When I couldn't find any evidence of her in my system with the information I had,

I took Bree's fingerprints and submitted them to the database but I haven't gotten the results back yet. While I was waiting, I figured it couldn't hurt. I guess you must've found the same article I did."

I took Detective Logan into the kitchen and showed him my laptop. The page was still open to the article I read. "Yep, that's the one," he said, straightening and unzipping his leather jacket. "You and I both think it looks like her."

"But it says she might have something to do with a robbery!"

"I have a bad feeling about this. I think her case might be less straightforward than a wrong place, wrong time, run-of-the-mill murder."

"Actually, there might be more of a problem than that," I told him. I reached into my purse and pulled out the envelope. "I also found this in Bree's apartment."

"What is it?"

"Take a look," I said, handing it to him.

Detective Logan shook open the envelope and the contents, now so familiar to me, fell into his hand. "Where did you find these?" he asked, glancing with visible curiosity at me. "I must have searched every square inch of her apartment!"

"They were taped under the drawer of her nightstand. She must have been trying to make sure no one found them."

"You did," pointed out Detective Logan. He opened the passport and compared it to the driver's license. "These look real enough to me but I'll have to send them to a specialist lab and get them checked out. I'm guessing Bree is short for Brittany and a nickname she regularly used."

"What about the money?"

Detective Logan turned the corners of several bills. "All the serial numbers are different so I think they're probably legit."

"I don't know if that's a good thing."

"I don't know either. Maybe she came by this money legitimately, maybe not. I'll need to take all of it for evidence."

"Of course."

"You said someone came into the apartment searching for something," said Detective Logan. "I doubt they were just looking for the passport. It wouldn't have been valuable to anyone else."

"Then what?"

"All I can say is, it's a good thing they didn't find you. I know I warned you before but I mean it this time: don't go back to Bree's apartment at all! Not for anything! I have a bad feeling about this case. I'm going to post someone at her place discreetly to watch it in the event that anyone comes back."

"I won't go back," I promised, sincerely intending not to.

"I mean it," warned Detective Logan. His eyes narrowed.

"I get the message," I told him.

"I better take these down to the police station. Is there anything else you thought of? Something you haven't told me? Anything that she might have said to you?"

"No," I replied. "But I'm not sure she would have told me anything true now."

"It seems like you're the only person who really knew Bree here."

"But I didn't. That's just it! I know that now."

"All the same, she talked to you and you worked together on a daily basis. You were the closest thing she had to a friend and you also managed to figure out where she hid this," he said, holding up the envelope.

"There is something else," I interjected before giving him a brief explanation of the photo on her mantel. I reached for the frame, which I handed to Detective Logan. "This photo was in her apartment and she said this couple were her parents, but I just picked this frame up in the New Treasures gift shop today and Grace said the snapshots were all stock models. This exact photo is supplied to all kinds of picture frames."

"It was probably part of Bree's plan. She wanted to look normal in case anyone came over," said Detective Logan.

"I was discussing her with a few friends and they all told me a different story about her background. I don't think she ever repeated the same thing to anyone. Do you think there was even a speck of truth in anything she said?"

"Maybe. We might never know," he answered. "I wish I could give you more to go on. Give me your friends' names and I'll look into it."

I gave him the names and repeated what Meredith Blake had said about the conversation she overheard. "Now at least I can guess why she was on the run," I said, feeling sad.

Detective Logan looked up as he finished writing in his notepad. "Doesn't seem like that much to run from in my view. Plenty of people have incurred petty crimes that stay on their records; and if there was only the sole occasion, I doubt she would even get jail time! Take care," he said as we moved to the front of the house. He opened the door and looked up toward the sky, wincing at the latest bout of rain as he zipped his jacket and turned his collar up. "Hey, I heard you're circulating a petition to save the library. Count me in and tell me where to sign," he added.

I smiled. "I will and thank you!" Closing the door quickly, I did not care to watch his retreating back especially when the outside cold was chilling my house. Detective Logan left me with a lot to think about. None of it made Bree sound like the desperate, fearful, young woman who was fleeing from abuse or the image I had painted in my head. It was a bit fanciful for me to jump to any conclusions about her, and even though I tried, I still couldn't believe she was the petty criminal that she now appeared to be.

The whole thing was too bizarre. I couldn't imagine why any criminal would pick my sleepy, little town as a hiding place; and as I thought that, the answer dawned on me. Who would have ever suspected her coming here? No one. I wouldn't. None of my friends ever felt the least bit suspicious of her, not until after her death.

I was glad I finally unloaded the burdensome envelope on Detective Logan but now I worried about the course the investigation was taking. Detective Logan correctly pointed out that Bree lied to me, and probably lied about every facet of her life. Yet, I still liked her. She was warm and friendly, always helped me, and was someone I easily trusted. Logan was convinced she was a liar through-and-through but surely, all these months couldn't have been just a huge, exhausting act? I remembered Logan's parting words; did Bree really have to hide out after only one theft? He was right. Plenty of people had petty crimes on their records and they didn't feel compelled to run away in order to conceal them. Yet Bree not only changed her name, but also created a false history, and sought a town where no one knew her. Could she have been part of something much bigger?

Logan was still seeking a murderer. Now that Bree's suspicious past was coming to light, did he really care anymore about why someone would've killed her? Did he still plan to locate her family?

I wasn't sure of the answer to those questions. Not positively. Perhaps it was best for Detective Logan to concentrate on making our town as safe as possible, but that didn't mean Bree's murder should be pushed aside.

It seemed that the only person still working on Bree's behalf now was me. I wasn't sure if I should itemize all the lies she told, but I wanted to.

Sitting down, I reached for my notepad to start making notes. I knew Bree's full name was Brittany Johnson. I had her photo. I could easily describe the way she looked the last time I saw her, even if that description were different from her driver's license photo. *The license!* I brightened. Although I'd already handed over that evidence to Detective Logan, I still had the picture on my phone, which meant I had her address.

There was a little time left before the library reopened. It was a long drive, but I could make the trip to the city. Plus, I was sure I'd be safe. If someone were looking for whatever they thought Bree was hiding here in Calendar, I would be much safer out of town.

It was too late to go there now and the idea of driving home in the dark on the highway didn't thrill me at all; but first thing tomorrow, I planned to drive to the city. I promised not to go back to Bree's apartment here in town but never said anything about her former residence. I could go to Bree's former address and ask around to learn more about her. Someone must have gotten a forwarding address for her or the person to call in the event of an emergency. It might have even been possible that Bree was still officially renting the apartment. If so, I felt sure I could talk my way inside.

There was also a huge library in the city that I wanted to visit too. A friend worked there. I was sure she could advise me on some strategies for saving the library. Plus, I knew they kept a digital stock of newspapers and I could search for more information about Bree. If anyone asked me why I went all the way to the city, that would be my cover.

Pleased at my swift decision, I decided to tackle some other things I didn't normally find the time to do. I tidied my kitchen and thoroughly cleaned the refrigerator before sorting through all the packets and cans in my cabinets. After aligning everything nicely and throwing away a few things past their expiration dates, I did my laundry and changed the bed linens. But despite how much I busied myself with the routine chores, Bree never left my mind.

CHAPTER TEN

A few minutes after eight o'clock, I got in my car and pulled out of the driveway. Overhead, the sky was gray and cloudy and the wind blew bitterly, but it wasn't raining. For that reason alone, I concluded today would be a good day. Putting my foot down, I powered along Maple View, reaching with one hand to switch on the radio.

The explosion almost made me lose control of the car. I grabbed the wheel with both hands and pulled hard to the left as I slammed on the brakes, spluttering to a halt at the side of the road. My knuckles were white as I clutched the wheel, breathing hard. After a moment, I looked up, wondering if anyone happened to notice my emergency stop. Fortunately, the area was clear.

Climbing out, I walked around the back of the car, my shoulders dropping when I saw the expected flat tire, and the reason for the explosion. No, not just flat, it was shredded. There was no way I could drive to the city on just three wheels. I never expected I would need to perform a tire change but I supposed I had to. Looking up, I thanked the sky for being clear and the sun for constantly trying to break through the clouds, even if it remained so cold.

Walking back around to the driver's seat, I leaned in and popped the trunk. I pulled the trunk lid up and checked out the spare tire before searching for the jack as a car rolled past.

"Everything okay?" asked a voice.

Glancing over my shoulder, I saw Jason Rees pulling up alongside me with his window down. *Was it my imagination or were his blue eyes sparkling?* I blinked, suddenly aware that he was awaiting my response.

"Flat tire," I said, pointing to the wretchedly traitorous wheel.

"Let me help you," he said. Before I could protest, Jason switched into reverse, skilfully parking his car behind mine. He hopped out and strode over.

"You really don't need to bother," I told him.

"What kind of man would I be if I left a lady stranded on the side of the road? Especially here, in the middle of nowhere?"

"My house is right over there." I pointed. "I'm literally less than a minute away from my driveway."

"My point stands. Hmm, it's no problem to get this tire off but your spare is flat," he said.

"You're kidding!" I groaned. It was bad enough that my tire blew out and now my spare was no better?! After Detective Logan left, I devoted the previous evening to planning out this day and I couldn't afford to waste any time. With the winter days still shortening, I was determined to start out early and be back home well before dark. Plus, I had to factor in a decent amount of time to prepare for my date with Tom. My dress was hanging in my bedroom and I had already organized my accessories but I still needed to take a bath and do my makeup. It was so long since my last date, I didn't know exactly how long it would take me to get ready and I needed some extra time for any errors in my judgment.

"I hate to deliver more bad news but this is a pretty bad blow-out. I think you should get a licensed mechanic to take a look at it and make sure your suspension hasn't been compromised."

I pulled a face. "That sounds very expensive and time-consuming."

"Sorry." Jason offered an apologetic smile. "Were you going very far?"

"Into the city. I thought I'd get an early start. I suppose I could catch the train." Mentally, I began to calculate the cost of a cab to the station, along with a return ticket, plus any other expenses I would incur while getting around the city.

"Why don't you just travel with me?" Jason surprised me by asking. "I have to head into the city for a meeting and I can drop you off wherever you need to go and pick you up later on my way back."

"Oh, no!" I shook my head vehemently. "No, I couldn't impose on you like that." Besides, I wasn't sure I wanted to spend two hours trapped in a car with Jason. *Each way.* He probably hoped to persuade me of all the benefits in shutting down the library and then we would have to get into an argument about it. Even thinking about it made me anxious.

"You're not imposing at all. We can keep each other company and if it makes you feel better, you can buy me breakfast on the way. So far, I'm being fueled solely on coffee."

"I..." I hesitated, looking toward my hobbled car then back at Jason's SUV. It looked so warm and comfortable, but more importantly, it had the crucial four wheels. If I took the train, it would add hours to my journey plus the cost of the train ticket and all the cab rides around the city. If Jason gave me a ride, all it would cost was his breakfast and a potential earache. I glanced at his SUV again, thinking how much I *really* wanted to see Bree's apartment.

"I promise not to talk about land development," said Jason as he smiled.

"Fine," I agreed. How bad could it be? Jason and I could listen to the radio, exchange a few pleasantries, and do exactly the same on the ride home. I turned my eyes to the rain clouds that were now hovering ominously overhead, eclipsing the rays of sunlight that kept trying to break though, and resolved that a ride with Jason beat taking the train. "Thank you, Jason. I really appreciate it."

"It's nothing, really. Grab your things and secure your car before we hit the road."

~

"You listen to rock music?" I said after the song finished. The car was pleasantly warm, and the heat thawed me out thoroughly. My coat and bag lay across the back seat.

Jason darted a glance at me. "You look surprised."

"I never thought of you as a Foo Fighters kind of guy."

The edges of Jason's lips struggled not to smile. "You actually think of me?"

"Only so much as you didn't strike me as a secret rocker."

"It's the suit, isn't it? You thought I liked classical music."

"Yes," I admitted. "Or possibly jazz." I resisted adding *pretentious jazz.*

"At least you didn't say pretentious jazz."

"I would never," I told him, biting my cheek.

"You're mocking me," he laughed. "Okay, I do like classical music and jazz. My mother insisted I practice piano every day for ten years. I have a good foundation in all kinds of music but I only started to play good music after I realized I could use all of that knowledge to play whatever I wanted to play. What about you? Do you play an instrument?"

I shook my head. "I wish I could, but unfortunately, I'm not inclined that way. The closest I came to music appreciation was creating a display at the library. It featured all the books that discussed different kinds of music. I am an enthusiastic listener, however."

"Do you listen to rock music?"

"That, and other genres."

"If I was still a kid, I'd make you a mixed tape of all my favorites."

I giggled, unable to constrain the sound. The last person I ever figured would offer to make me a mixed tape was Jason Rees, but he seemed so genuine. I darted a quick look at him, assuming that a lot of girls probably longed for him to make them a mixed tape back in high school.

"There's a diner coming up on the right. You hungry?"

"Starving," I admitted as I felt a familiar rumble starting in my belly. Luckily, it ended before making itself known over the sound of the music.

"Great. I always stop here on this route. They have the best pie."

"You eat pie for breakfast?"

"It's one of the nicest things about being an adult. No more food rules."

"Sometimes I only eat ice cream for supper," I admitted, smiling again. The conversation began a little stilted, but true to his promise, Jason never talked shop. Instead, he remained warm and engaging.

"Don't forget chocolate sauce! Gotta cover all the food groups." Jason turned the car off the highway and directed it down the ramp, taking the next right turn and following a road that curved around before running parallel to the highway we just exited. After a couple minutes, he pulled into the lot, parking in front of the diner.

"I think we hit the breakfast rush," said Jason, nodding at all the cars in the lot. "Let's get inside before those clouds dump all the rain they're holding. I have to say, I preferred it when it was snowing."

I grabbed my jacket from the back seat and tucked it around my shoulders. The rain began spitting just as we hurried inside. Most of the booths were taken up with families, couples, and friends and the counter was also full. Jason nodded to a booth he spotted near the back. "Let's sit down there."

"Good morning, you two," said the smiling waitress as she approached us with two menus and a freshly made pot of coffee. "Don't often see you with company, Jason."

"Dee, this is Sara," Jason said. "I'm giving Sara a ride to the city, and thought I'd show her my favorite place to eat on the way."

"Hi," I said, raising my hand to give her a small wave.

"Hi, Sara. Coffee?"

"Please."

"I'll give you two a moment to decide what you want," said Dee, looking up as the doors opened and a pair of police officers stepped inside. I tensed for a moment but when they looked away, I soon relaxed.

"No need on my account. Pancakes and bacon," I decided after quickly scanning the menu.

"Sounds good. Make that two," Jason said.

"No pie?" I teased.

"Maybe on the way back to Calendar."

"Pancakes and bacon coming up," said Dee, making a note on her pad. She gave us one last smile before heading off to greet the new customers.

"So why were you driving into the city?" asked Jason. He plucked a packet of sugar from the complimentary basket and ripped open the top, stirring it into his cup.

"I'm visiting someone," I told him, keeping it deliberately vague.

"Family?"

"No, all my family lives in Calendar. This is a friend. I have another day off from work so I thought I'd make the trip for something to do."

"Sounds like a nice way to spend the day," said Jason, without commenting on why I had another day off.

"I hope so," I said, trying to ignore my niggling guilt for telling a lie. I couldn't tell Jason the truth. He'd probably turn around and drive directly to the Calendar Police Department to suggest Detective Logan start investigating instead. He would definitely not drop me on Bree's former doorstep and I needed him to do exactly that. There was no other way I could find out who Bree really was. I hastily directed Jason to another topic. "Why are you going to the city?" I asked.

"Couple of meetings. Nothing important," he said, shrugging off the question.

Immediately, my nerves jangled. Hearing the casual nature of his answer, I knew it had something to do with the library, and I was sure of it. But if I asked him, I feared it would only spark another argument. I didn't want to annoy Jason into leaving me there, no matter how pleasant the diner was, and I also didn't want the rest of our journey to be awkwardly endured under a tense silence. The best thing to do now was not to ask. I could always grill him on the way home. By that time, his meetings would have concluded and he'd be riper for offering more satisfying answers.

"I hope it isn't too arduous," I said, settling on politeness.

"I was planning to head back to Calendar around three," he said, ending the conversation easily and just as politely. "Does that give you enough time to visit your friend?"

"Plenty."

"Do you get into the city often?" he asked.

I shook my head. "Not as often as I'd like to. I keep thinking I'll come here and see the sights, or maybe do some shopping, but I always find enough to do in Calendar and besides, the city will always be there..." I trailed off, thinking that Bree had no idea when her last day would be. If she had, would she have done anything differently? "I should stop putting it off," I decided out loud.

"Maybe you'll get time today… after you see your friend?"

Dee appeared beside the booth with a plate in each hand. "Pancakes for two. You'll find flatware in the basket and maple syrup in that jug. Wave a hand if I can get you anything else."

We thanked her and my eyes widened at the huge plate stacked with thick pancakes and crispy bacon. I inhaled, closing my eyes briefly and letting the sugary scent invade my nostrils. When I opened my eyes, Jason was watching me. "Wait until you actually try them," he said knowingly, his face lighting up with a boyish smile.

"What if I'm disappointed after so much of a build-up?"

"Don't worry, you won't be." Jason cut off a triangular bite of pancakes and bit into it, making a pleased and satisfied sound.

Taking the hint that our conversation was temporarily over, I followed his example. One bite quickly followed another and I'd already finished a whole pancake before

I ever reached for the syrup. "These are the best pancakes ever!" I groaned. "How could I not know about this place?"

"We regulars keep it quiet so you non-regulars don't eat all our good food."

"You can't keep this diner a secret. It's not fair to ... to... the rest of the world!" I finished, unashamed of my dramatic proclamation.

"Yeah? I bet you come back before you even mention it to another soul."

"You said something about us stopping by on the way home too," I pointed out, waving a forkful of pancakes at him. Jason followed the fork with his eyes. I dropped it into my mouth before he could think about eating it and he laughed.

"I meant it. You need to try the homemade pie."

I chewed a piece of bacon and swallowed. If the pie was as good as their breakfast pancakes, I knew I was in for a good time. "I'm already looking forward to it," I clucked happily.

We continued to talk about this and that as we finished our breakfasts and accepted coffee refills from Dee. Our conversation drifted between childhood memories and all the things we enjoyed the most and I soon found myself relaxing further. Jason was easy to talk to, not to mention, charming and funny. By the time I settled the bill, insisting it really was my treat since he was kind enough to give me a lift, I couldn't remember why he annoyed me in the beginning. I liked this Jason. He was quick and knowledgeable and I couldn't deny how nice he was to look at.

We continued to talk as we drove but after a while, I realized Jason wasn't paying attention.

"Jason?"

"Hmm?"

"You didn't hear a word I said," I admonished him, feeling uncomfortable.

"I did. I... uh..." Jason grimaced. "You're right, I didn't. Sorry."

"Is something else on your mind?"

"No, it's..." Jason frowned and shook his head. "It's probably nothing," he finished with a dissatisfied huff.

"What is it?"

"I think we're being followed," he said, and I sensed the disbelief seeping into his voice.

"Followed? By whom?"

"I don't know... Don't turn around!" he insisted when I began to look over my shoulder. I quickly pressed the back of my head against the headrest, preventing me from turning it.

"What makes you think we're being followed?"

"Check your rearview mirror. There's a black sedan about three cars back. I didn't think anything of it until a few minutes ago."

"There must be thousands of black sedans."

"I think they've been trailing us since we left Calendar."

"It can't be the same car."

"I think it is. I noticed it a few miles out of town but ignored it since there aren't that many on and off ramps before the diner. I didn't see them come into the parking lot after we did, but I noticed them again when we got back on the highway. They've been three cars behind us ever since."

"Why would someone be following you?"

"What makes you think they're following *me?*"

"Because! It's your car!" I pointed out, my voice rising.

"I'm not the only one in it!"

I thought about that for a little bit. I didn't know Jason nearly well enough to suggest a valid reason for someone to follow him but maybe property developers attracted the wrong sort of crowd. There might have been a good reason to follow me. I discovered Bree's body. I also found her documents right before someone else turned over her apartment while possibly looking for the same thing. Detective Logan pointed out that I probably knew her best. Did they think I knew something? *What if they wanted to know what I did next?* I gulped. If that were the case, we were leading them directly to the next clue. The only problem? I could hardly tell Jason that!

"If you're worried," I suggested, trying to keep my tone casual despite the worry that nearly overwhelmed me, "why don't we try to lose them?"

"That might be a good idea." Jason paused, thinking. "We're almost at the city limits. I'm not going to do anything until we enter the city. I don't think there's any way we can ditch them until then. As soon as we're off the highway, I think I can shake them without looking like we're trying to get rid of them."

"Sounds good to me."

He frowned hard. "I must sound paranoid."

"You just sound worried."

Jason flashed me a grateful smile. "Thanks for not saying I'm being ridiculous."

I forced a cheerful smile. "What's the worst that could happen? We have a story to tell now. Remember that time we were chased by a mysterious black sedan?"

"One for the grandkids?" Jason laughed. "Being chased might be an exaggeration."

"It's not a story though without a car chase. I should know!"

"Maybe that could be your next display? Exciting adventures that also feature car chases."

This time, I smiled for real. "Actually, I like that idea."

"The off ramp is up ahead. Ready?"

"Ready," I replied.

Jason kept the speed at an even pace and we took the exit ramp, gliding towards the city. As we approached the changing lights, he floored the engine and sailed right through. Resisting the urge to turn and look back, I monitored the car from the wing mirror. "They got stuck behind the car in front of them," I told him.

"Great. Let's put as much distance between us now as we can. You know, it probably really is nothing," he added.

"Absolutely," I agreed. Before Jason returned his attention to the road, I glimpsed a look of worry that told me he thought it was anything but. Jason really believed someone was following us, and the more I thought about it, the more I had to agree with him. I just wished I knew what they wanted.

CHAPTER ELEVEN

"Are you sure this is the correct address?"

The building formerly belonging to Bree, or rather, Brittany Johnson, seemed very similar to the neighboring properties, meaning, it was terribly rundown. Looking neglected and dejected, the old paint on the shop sign was peeling and piles of litter cluttered the adjacent stairwell. The first floor housed a shabby-looking pawn shop, and the signs in the grilled window offered cash on the spot. I guessed they didn't always run the necessary background checks and consequently, some of the goods inside were on the hotter end of the temperature scale. Display cases facing the street showed electrical equipment and jewelry, along with a mixture of curios. I looked over at the building and searched for a number, eventually finding it painted on the wall by the staircase. Yes, it was the right building.

"This is it," I told him, wondering how the prim Bree that I knew could have lived here. In the daylight, it didn't seem so bad but I could only wonder what the neighborhood might have been like at night. I glanced up at the street lamps nearby. Two had smashed bulbs. Definitely not a good sign.

"I can wait," Jason offered as two young men with their hoods pulled up over their heads walked past. One flicked the end of a cigarette into the street. They continued further down the street, turning the corner at the crossroads.

"No, that's fine. I'll be okay," I hoped.

"Are you sure?" He hesitated, then continued, "I don't mean to be a pain but this isn't the nicest area. If you want me to stick around while you visit your friend, I can postpone my meeting."

"No, really, I'm fine." I waved him off, acting far more jovial than I felt. "I'm just going to visit for a short time; then I'll call an Uber and run some errands. Where shall I meet you?"

Jason thought about it, then replied, "Why don't we meet at the public library?"

That suited me fine since I planned to visit there anyway. "I know where it is."

"I really don't mind..."

"Go!" I told him, and this time, I was waving impatiently as I reached for the door and popped the handle. It was sweet of Jason to be so concerned but I really wanted him to leave. The black sedan he spotted had shaken me up. Even though we apparently managed to lose them, I didn't want Jason sticking around. If they were following me, and had even an inkling of where I was going, Jason's SUV would stand out like a lighthouse on the street. It was much better for us both if he left. Plus, I could hardly question the neighbors if he were hanging around and acting like my bodyguard. Jason exuded the kind of professional air that could be off-putting to anyone who did know Bree or that she had something to hide. I, on the other hand, took great care to look as wholesome as possible, dressing in blue jeans, a cream knit sweater and my thick, winter coat.

"If you need a ride, call me. I'm still not sure about leaving you here. I don't like it." He glanced around, as if he expected a group of thugs to hijack us at any moment. Unfortunately, that thought had already crossed my mind.

"'Fraid you're going to have to like it," I told him, plastering on a cheerful smile to mask my worries. "See you later!" I pushed the door closed before he could protest, waving as I took off for the stairwell. Tightening my coat around me, I took the first step, and popped my collar up against the frigid wind.

At the half landing, I turned and waved again. Jason raised his hand in return. I watched him slide the SUV out of the parking space, and a moment later, he was lost from view. I wasn't sure whether to heave a sigh of relief or be worried that I was now completely alone. Turning towards the ascent, I took a deep breath and continued upwards. Only one door led from this floor. I craned my head up and saw another door leading from the stairway on the floor above. An "A" was stenciled in yellow paint on the outside; the hue contrasting unpleasantly with the brown door.

Sounds from a television came from the inside. I raised my hand and knocked, hoping someone would answer. The license was just a few months old, and Bree arrived in Calendar only three months ago. Since she kept the license, those two things made me sure this had to have been her last address.

I could hear footsteps inside getting closer and I suddenly realized how foolish it was to assume Bree had a roommate. What did I plan to do if she lived alone? Or if her apartment had already been rented to someone else? Did I plan to pick the lock with absolutely no experience in doing so and break in? I had definitely read one too many mystery novels!

"Yeah?" said the young woman who answered the door. Despite the cold, she was wearing a black top with one sleeve, a shabby leather vest, and skinny, black jeans. A blast of warm air flowed out the door. I took a closer look at the sleeve, and saw it was actually a full arm tattoo of leopard spots. She gave me a head to toe look that instantly conveyed her annoyance and suspicion.

"Hi. Does Bree... I mean, Brittany, still live here?" I asked, trying not to stare at the ink as I assumed this woman probably didn't know Bree by the name I knew her.

"Brittany Johnson?" The woman raised her eyebrows. "She used to. You don't look like you're from the law."

"I'm not," I hurried to assure her, flashing the palms of my hands in visual surrender. "She hasn't done anything wrong."

The woman snorted. "Then what do you want?"

"I'm her cousin," I said, scrambling for a plausible lie. "I was in town and I thought I'd come by for a quick visit. It's been a long time."

"Well, you're three months too late. Brittany just up and split one day without a word. At least she left me two weeks rent instead of stiffing me for the whole lot." She leaned against the door frame, taking her time to look me over more closely. Her gaze wasn't particularly friendly but not unfriendly either.

"Oh. Do you possibly know where she went?"

The woman lifted her inked shoulder and let it drop again. "No, I don't know. Don't care either. I'm glad to see the last of her."

"I'm sorry to..."

I stopped as the woman cut me off, apparently eager to unload her annoyance at Bree's sudden departure on me. "I don't want to see anymore of her so-called friends around here neither. Or, as I prefer to call them, creeps. This might not be the best neighborhood, but we don't need to make it any worse." She gave me a very pointed look. I glanced down at my jacket and jeans. I didn't think I looked like a creep but perhaps her definition varied from mine.

"What do you mean?" I asked.

"Those guys she runs around with. I think one might have been her boyfriend but he seemed like a real nasty piece of work, if you know what I mean."

"Uh-huh," I murmured, hoping she would just tell me what she meant exactly.

"Always wore flashy suits, turning up at all times of the day and night, picking Bree up for some kind of job. I asked her once if he was asking her do anything nasty but she said no. I was kind of worried about her for a while," she finished.

"Do you know who he is?"

"She never called him by a name, just his nickname, Tricky."

"Do you know where Tricky lives?"

"No, I thought she might have run off with him, but when he came around a week after Bree walked out of here, I told him to never come back or bring his creepy buddy around either."

"Why was he so creepy?" I wondered.

"Always staring at me but he hardly ever spoke. Bree said he was okay but he gave me the jitters. I'll bet twenty bucks his mugshot is hanging up in a U.S. Post Office somewhere."

"That sounds awfully worrying."

"You said it, sister."

I pursed my lips, wondering what to make of that information. "Do you know where I could find her family? Her mom, Maybe?"

A cloud of suspicion reappeared on the woman's face. "I thought you were her cousin?"

"I am; but like I said, it's been such a long time. I wasn't sure if her mom was still around, or her dad."

"I don't know anything about her dad, but her mom dumped her in foster care when she was twelve. Brittany said her mom told her she'd gotten too pretty and she didn't want her hanging around her boyfriend. Couldn't deal with the competition." I pulled a face and leopard woman continued, "I know, right? What a bitch! I think Brittany was lucky. You must know all of that though."

"Not all, just some of it," I mumbled, hoping she wouldn't ask me to clarify anything. The story was quite different from Bree's scant description of two hard-working parents who strove to give her a happy home and healthy upbringing. Perhaps it was something she created to survive the grim reality of her early years. I couldn't blame her. "I guess Brittany chose not to keep in touch with any members of her family at all."

"None that I ever met. And Brittany lived here for a whole year."

"I might inquire at the last place where she worked. I think she said it was a bookshop. Do you have the address by any chance?"

Leopard woman shook her head. "Brittany never said anything about a bookshop! No, she kept some real strange hours. I think she worked for Tricky. And I'm damned if I'll ever ask what kinda weird shit he was into! I sincerely doubt it was legal and that's more than I want to know. I don't recommend that you find out either. Listen, I gotta go, but if you catch up to Brittany, you can give her this." Leopard woman stooped down and grabbed a large box from behind the door, which she thrust into my arms. "I was going to give it to Goodwill but since you're related and all, maybe you can meet up with her somewhere and pass it along."

"Oh, I don't..." I started to say as she released the weight of the box into my arms.

"And tell Brittany not to bother coming back! I already rented her room to someone more reliable without any creepo pals." With that, she pushed the door shut, leaving me to stare at the brown wood with the yellow stencil, then down at the box.

There was no way I could take the box with me. It was far too heavy and cumbersome, and Bree no longer needed anything inside it. Never mind the potential issue of Jason asking me what was in it. I couldn't take it with me but I could sure look through it.

Stepping away from the door, I set it down on the stairwell floor. I opened the flaps, peering inside. There were a few dog-eared paperbacks and some cheap trinkets. A scarf, a single glove, and some unmatched mugs. I poked around further and withdrew a notepad with sheets of newspaper fluttering between the leaves. As I lifted it out a photo slipped from it, landing on the floor. I reached for it, frowning at the obvious tear line. Bree looked much younger in the photo. Her hair was longer and she was smiling. An arm hung casually around her shoulders, obviously not hers, but the rest of the man was missing. Something was written on his lower arm. No, not written. I squinted more closely at it. It was a very good tattoo of a scorpion, inked on the topside of his wrist, and the tail curling under. The scorpion held a diamond between its pincers.

If Bree had ripped the photo in half, she clearly didn't want to be reminded of him. That made me wonder if the man could possibly be the *creepy Tricky* or someone else.

Keeping the photo in hand, I opened the notepad. Most of the pages had indecipherable scribbling and doodles but what I glimpsed between the leaves attracted my attention.

Bree had clipped several articles from national newspapers. *The New York Post* clipping had a short piece about a heist from a jewelry store, which said the thieves made off with two hundred thousand dollars in jewels. The story in *The Washington Post* featured a suspected group of thieves who used a distraction technique to walk out with fifty thousand dollars in watches. *The Connecticut Mirror* described a smash-and-grab worth sixty-two thousand dollars, while the *Atlantic City Weekly* covered a gang known for forging and cashing in chips around town.

There were sixteen clippings, every one describing unsolved thefts.

I shuffled them around and put them in order by date, noting that the smaller robberies were the oldest, while the newer ones had the highest values. The most recent occurred a little over three months ago. It involved a two million-dollar haul of gems, cut and uncut rubies, emeralds, and diamonds.

Why would Bree want to keep all of these articles?

I searched through the box but found nothing else of interest so I stuffed the articles and photo into my pocket.

Downstairs was the pawn shop. If Bree needed money to leave town fast, perhaps she'd have gone to someplace like that, where few questions would be asked to get it. I left the box on the stairwell and hurried downstairs to the pawn shop. A bell jangled as the door opened and a bearded man sitting by the register looked up. He blinked at me, then looked back down at the newspaper on the glass counter.

I took a few minutes to examine the dusty shelves, spotting instruments, electronics, and other things people didn't need as much as they needed cash. As I browsed slowly, I got the impression that I was being watched.

"You looking for something in particular?" asked the man after a couple of minutes.

"I'm not sure," I said, crossing the store and passing a fairly decent bicycle and some old pieces of furniture. There was nothing, however, that I could identify as Bree's. "My friend, Bree... uh, Brittany, used to live upstairs and I thought she might have sold something here."

"Brittany?" He frowned. "Dark-haired gal? Haven't seen her in a while. Think she moved out."

"That's right," I agreed. "About three months ago. Did she pawn anything around that time?"

"Nope," he said. "Don't think she never had nothing to pawn."

I resisted the urge to correct his grammar, asking instead, "What about her boyfriend?"

"What are you? A cop?" He laughed at his own suggestion.

"No, just her cousin. I've been looking for her."

His face softened. "So was the boyfriend. Came in mad as hell, asking lotsa questions about her. Don't think she told him she went."

"No, I don't think she did."

"Good thing too," he said with a grunt, his face hard again.

"What do you mean?"

He opened his mouth before he seemed to think better of it. "We don't want no trouble here."

"Of course not. Thank you for your help." I knew I wouldn't get anything more out of him. He was too suspicious and I was clearly asking the wrong questions. Plus, he seemed scared of the mysterious Tricky, although he most definitely was not scared of me.

"She never pawned nothing," he said when I reached the door. "But she did come in looking for something just before she left."

"Oh?"

He leaned over and tapped the glass case that formed the counter. I stepped over, curious, and he folded back his newspaper. Underneath the case were several guns, and I noticed the case was locked. "She looked at these?"

"She did but she never bought one," he told me. "Lotsa paperwork for these. Can't sell 'em without it."

"Did she say why she needed a gun?" I asked, wondering just how afraid Bree might have been when she ran away from her life.

"No, and I never asked."

"Thank you," I told him again and this time, I left.

Outside on the sidewalk, I checked the street for other vehicles and anyone who might have been watching me. Between the car possibly tailing us, the leopard woman and the pawn shop guy, I had plenty of reasons to feel jittery. However, the street seemed average and ordinary. A young couple with a stroller passed by, then a woman pushing a shopping cart shuffled past me.

I activated my phone, sending a request for a car to Bree's former address. A few minutes passed before an Uber rolled up. I climbed in and we drove towards downtown. Every so often, I turned to check behind us but saw no black sedan following us.

CHAPTER TWELVE

Even though my search online could not provide a bookshop in the location where Bree had listed her reference, I wanted to physically check it out. The Uber dropped me off at the location where it was supposed to be and I stepped out. The sun was bright but still cold, and the temperature was only fractionally warmer than when I left my house four hours earlier. Thanks to Jason's suggestion that we eat breakfast at the diner, I wasn't hungry yet and took my time walking the two blocks each way.

The downtown area had nicer shops than Bree's former neighborhood. A general mix of chain restaurants and fashion stores, along with some independently-owned shops sprinkled amidst the small businesses. The traffic flowed steadily in both directions and the pedestrians were mainly comprised of older people and parents with small children. I guessed that everyone else was either at school or work. That was where I would have been too, if not for Bree's murder.

A stationery shop now occupied the address of Bree's supposed bookshop. I stepped inside and looked around at the tables, which were stacked with pretty notepads and pencils. All the supplies were bright and pretty rather than the usual, boring, standard office inventory. If I hadn't already bought my mother's birthday gift, I could easily have found her something here.

"Can I help you?" asked a short lady with straight, black hair, cut severely at her shoulders. She adjusted her thick-rimmed, black glasses as she asked her question.

"Have you been here long?" I asked.

"Six months," she said.

"Oh." I frowned, attempting to look puzzled. "My friend, Brittany, said there was a bookshop here."

"Nope, just us," she said, without any indication to suggest she recognized the name I just mentioned.

"Perhaps it was next door?" I noticed a vacant store adjacent to this one.

"No, I think that used to be a clothing store," she said. "They were only open a few months before they abruptly closed down."

"What a shame. Was that recently?"

"Yeah, only a few weeks ago. They definitely didn't sell any books though."

"And there are no bookshops around here at all?"

"There's a library, but that's a good three blocks north," the lady replied. "We carry a small selection of children's books, if that's any help?"

"Thanks, but no. I was actually looking for someone that worked there, rather than for a bookshop, itself." I paused. Why didn't I think of that before? I had a photo of Bree! The one from the box I'd been informally assigned to remove. I reached into my pocket, pulling out the wad of newspaper articles and the photo. Shoving all the articles back into my pocket, I held out the photo. "Perhaps you recognize her? The photo's a little old," I explained as she studied it, "but she still looks the same."

"No, I'm sorry, I don't think I've ever seen her before," she said, shaking her head and returning the photo. I was watching her as she examined the photo and became slightly disappointed when she failed to show even a flicker of recognition. With a sinking feeling, I realized I'd been on a wild goose chase.

"Thanks for your time," I told her before leaving. I called another Uber, and began heading to the central library. Sinking into the backseat, I tried not to feel too disheartened. I was glad I followed the lead, even though it turned out to be a dead end. At least, the apartment gave me some promising clues but I wasn't sure what to do with some of the information. Like the stuff about Tricky and his creepy friends, or the gun Bree once considered purchasing but ultimately left town without. I debated over calling Detective Logan, but later decided I didn't want to risk annoying him with my limited investigation. He'd been very clear when he told me to stay away from Bree's apartment and I was pretty sure he wouldn't be pleased about my continuing to look into her past.

As we drove through the city, I pulled out the articles, smoothing out the somewhat crumpled paper to read again. What could have interested Bree so much in these articles? The one thing they had in common was that they were all thefts. By the time we pulled up to the curb in front of the library, I also learned that in each theft, the prime suspects were gang members working together to pull off the heists. However, none of the articles offered any information about how they might have accomplished them.

I paid the Uber driver and began the search for my friend. Back in my college days, I interned at the library one long summer. A woman named Mary Ruth was my mentor, and she cheerfully instructed me on all of the practical applications for working in a library. We'd kept in touch over the years and I was happy to see her now.

"This is such a nice surprise!" said Mary Ruth. Moving around the counter, she reached out to embrace me. "I doubt this is purely a social visit, however. You sounded so worried when you called."

"Is there somewhere we can talk?"

"Sure. I'm due for my lunch break so we can go someplace quiet." As Mary Ruth and I walked into her office, a part of the library that was off limits to patrons, I explained what happened to Bree at the Calendar Library. I also told her what I'd subsequently discovered. When I finished, she asked, "Do you think she came to your town for no good reason?"

"I'm not sure. At first, I suspected she could be hiding from someone who wanted to hurt her. Now I think she might have been hiding from someone she was involved with, and possibly, in a criminal way. She had a checkered past."

"It does sound like she might have fallen afoul with the wrong people." Mary Ruth gestured for me to take a seat on the battered, old, leather couch. "I'm not sure how I can be of any help though?"

"I wanted to take a quick look at some of the digital files. I was hoping to find something about Bree, maybe the reason why she thought all of these articles were worth keeping." I handed the articles to Mary Ruth.

"I doubt you'll find anything about that young lady. It would be like looking for a needle in a haystack, but these might be a possibility." Mary Ruth read through the clippings quickly but I felt sure she took everything in. She was a smart and efficient reader with an excellent memory. "I remember this one," she said, holding up one clipping. "It caused quite a commotion."

"What do you mean?" I asked, reaching for the article. Mary Ruth was referring to the latest one, the only one missing a newspaper name.

"It happened right here in the city," she said. "It made big news. The jewelry store in question caters to a very wealthy crowd. If I remember correctly, the thieves were reportedly a team of criminals; and the general consensus was that they scoped the store out many weeks before they actually robbed it."

"It says here that they stole uncut jewels as well as cut jewels. Uncut means they weren't already set into the various pieces of jewelry?"

"That's correct. There's some lovely books all about jewels and jewelry that you'll find on the third floor if you have enough time. It's not mentioned in the article but the report I heard on the news said that the gang got away with a lot of ready-made pieces like earrings, necklaces and so on, but they also managed to get inside a vault and stole the uncut pieces too. Apparently, after kidnapping the manager and forcing him to open the vault, the gang left him there, still tied up."

"How awful!"

"That's not even the worst part. The gang also left someone with his family just in case he tried to double-cross them in any way."

My jaw dropped. "That's horrible!"

"Not a gang you wanna mess with. Anyway, the news reports came to the same conclusion as the article. No one was ever caught."

"Do you think there's a link to these, or some way that they could be connected?" I asked, spreading the articles between us.

"It seems like it. Maybe your friend saw the connections between them."

"What if she actually knew who was behind it?" I wondered. "That would have given her a good reason to skip town and hide out."

"Doesn't explain why someone would have murdered her."

"No, not exactly, but maybe this gang was desperate to keep her quiet. They might have assumed she could decide at anytime to report them."

"That would be quite a story to take to the police, especially without any evidence."

I thought about that. Mary Ruth was right; Bree would have no guarantee the police would believe her. I felt sure she wouldn't dare risk the chance of blowing her cover without first receiving the assurance that she would be taken seriously. The very fact that she was living under an assumed name would already have established her as a liar, which wasn't a good start.

Meredith's words drifted back to my mind. What did Bree say about laying low somewhere on a beach? Those didn't sound like the words of a fugitive who was prepared to tell the police everything. It sounded more like she wanted to keep hiding just as much as the members of the gang did. It left a very troubling taste in my mouth.

"Sara?"

"Hmm? Yes?" I momentarily failed to realize Mary Ruth was talking.

"I asked if you wanted to see the digital archives?"

"Yes, please," I said, smiling. I didn't want my friend to know how worried I really was.

"Follow me."

The digital archives were housed in a room on the other side of the library. Two banks of long desks held several computers and the room was empty when we arrived. "Sometimes, we get students in here, or other scholarly types," Mary Ruth explained, "but it's usually quiet around this time. I'll show you how to operate the machines. I think you'll find them a lot easier than searching micro-fiche. Isn't technology a wonderful tool?"

I agreed it was. Mary Ruth showed me how to operate the search engine as well as how to refine the parameters and narrow it down to certain dates and/or locations. After practicing on my own a couple of times, and refreshing my memory, she excused herself, but not before reminding me to be sure to say goodbye when I left.

I first tried entering Bree's name, using all kinds of different combinations of her first and last names. I even tried different spellings but each search came up empty. Next, I sought more information about the robberies. However, excluding the final theft, the one that Mary Ruth recalled, there weren't any follow-up stories. There was also no trace of any connection between the thefts. The last theft turned out to be the biggest of all. Owing to its violent and audacious conduct, it spurred several more stories, each generally regurgitating the last until there was no new information to print.

Finally, I searched for any other similar thefts but the results didn't tell me anything that I hadn't already lifted from Bree's sad box of private possessions.

Resting back in my chair, I sighed. It was a good idea to try the searches but I knew I was defeated. I sent a simple text to Jason, telling him I was free whenever he was before I left to find Mary Ruth so I could say goodbye to her while I waited.

~

"How was your day?"

I jumped, blinking back into reality when I found Jason standing at my side. I leaned against the thick, brick balustrade leading up the steps to the library. I'd been enjoying a pleasant few minutes of people watching. Apparently, I missed seeing the one person I'd actually been waiting for.

"Sorry, I didn't mean to startle you. Are you okay?"

"I'm fine," I said, laughing at my reaction. Tension drained from me instantly. "I was temporarily lost in a world of my own. What did you say?"

"I asked how was your day? Did you have a nice visit?"

"Not what I expected," I told him truthfully, "but definitely interesting. How was your meeting?"

"Like any other. Everyone talked too much before we made new appointments for more meetings." Jason rolled his eyes and I laughed.

"I don't think I could work all day in an office," I admitted. "Too much bureaucracy."

"Tell me about it! I'm sure your day must have been better than mine. Did you have lunch?"

"I forgot to!" I patted my stomach and stifled a hunger pang. "Breakfast filled me up but now I'm sort of hungry again."

"My boss took me out for lunch and I could only push the salad around with my fork." Jason mimed doing just that. "I might have room for pie on the way back to Calendar although I'm in no hurry to leave if you aren't."

"Afraid the small town boredom will infect you if you get there too soon?" I teased.

Jason laughed. "Not at all. Calendar is a great town! Not at all boring! I bet there's a lot brewing under the surface that most people don't know about."

"I'm not so sure about that. The town gossips are masters at their job."

"I guess they must have their hands full now. Oh, I'm sorry!" He stopped suddenly as my face fell. "I didn't mean to be so crass. I wasn't implying your friend's death was fodder for gossip."

"I'm pretty sure that's all everyone is gossiping about," I told him, placing a hand on his arm to show him I didn't take any offense. I didn't get the impression Jason intended to imply anything or suggest more than how small town gossip worked. "There isn't much too tell, unfortunately."

"Detective Logan doesn't have any leads yet?"

"I don't think so."

"What about Bree's family? They must be very upset."

"I don't think she had any. Or, at least, she wasn't in touch with any family members," I said. I began thinking about how Bree's former roommate described her upbringing. Even if Detective Logan tracked someone down, I wasn't sure anyone would care enough about Bree to claim her body. That was a sad thought.

"That's too bad," said Jason. I nodded in agreement, and the two of us stood in silence for a moment.

"I have two brothers and two sisters," he said, surprising me. "I'm the youngest and my parents are still married."

"Really?"

"Which part?"

"All of it."

"Then, yes, really. Shall we go inside?" Jason indicated the public library that I exited from only a few minutes before. "Or shall we take the car?"

"Let's go inside," I told him. "There's a nice exhibition I was looking at when you called to say you were almost here."

"Lead the way." Jason held out his arm and I took it, pleased and surprised at the gallant gesture. "Are you and your family locals?" he asked as we stepped inside.

"You mean from Calendar? Yes. My mother lives there. My father passed away a few years ago."

"I'm sorry."

"You keep saying that."

"That I'm sorry? I suppose I do. I just can't keep from putting my foot in my mouth."

"Don't start licking your toes." I laughed at Jason's puzzled frown. "That's what my dad used to say whenever my mom or I put our feet in our mouths. I don't have any siblings. I would have liked at least one, I think. I envy you for having all of yours."

"I can lend you one or two," he joked. "I envy you too. You never had to share toys or a bedroom."

"I envy you always having someone to play with."

"I envy you never having to wear hand-me-downs."

"No way! You wore your sisters' clothes?" I gasped in mock shock as I deliberately took his comment literally.

"Only until college," he quipped, just as sharply.

We passed a pleasant hour, walking around the library and browsing the exhibition. I picked up a couple of paperbacks from the used sale shelf, and Jason waited with his arm again. He was always ready with something new to point out to me or to make an interesting comment regarding the architecture or history of the grand, old building. It felt nice to walk arm-in-arm, almost like we were a couple. The more I relaxed, the less I thought about Bree, or the man in her apartment, or the car following us. I didn't even notice the time until

139

Jason checked his watch. He announced we would have to leave soon if we intended to sample the famous pie and still get home before the night closed in. As he said it, I must admit a little ripple of guilt fluttered through me. Not only did I almost forget about my date with Tom, but I still needed to be home in time to take a bath and get dressed.

"Is it wrong if I say that I'm glad your car blew a tire?" Jason asked as we rolled to a stop in front of my house. That was a good three hours, and two large slices of pie, later.

"If it is, then I'm guilty too," I replied. "The journey just wouldn't have been the same alone."

"Truer words could not be said," agreed Jason. "You're pretty good company, Sara."

A blush started to fill my cheeks. "I would never have enjoyed the best pancakes in the world without you. Or the best pie."

"See? I have my perks." He paused, glanced away, then turned back again, and I frowned at the sudden shyness I saw in him again. "I'd like to take you to dinner if you don't have any plans tonight."

I winced involuntarily.

"Oh!" Jason sucked in a breath like I slapped him and his cheeks turned red. "I read that wrong. I thought... Of course, you don't want to go to dinner with me. I'm the one who's..."

"No, no," I interrupted him before he mentioned the library and reminded me of exactly how we knew each other. My hand drifted to his arm and I leaned in. "It's nothing to do with that. It's just that I made other dinner plans already."

"A date?" he asked, his voice cooler.

"Something like that," I said, strangely unwilling to say *yes, exactly that*.

"Lucky guy," said Jason. He climbed out of the car and walked around to my side, opening the door for me and offering his hand. I stepped down, like I was stepping out of a chariot, not an SUV, and Jason was the prince, not the developer who planned to ruin my library. "Good night, Sara."

"Good night, Jason," I said, wondering why I was so reluctant to let go of his hand.

CHAPTER THIRTEEN

"You look gorgeous." Tom's eyes swept over me, and a rush of embarrassed warmth filled me. "I feel like I won the lottery!"

"Oh, stop!" I chided him, secretly pleased at the unfamiliar praise. I'd made a substantial effort for my first date. Something that had taken far too long, if the brunch with Jason didn't count. Of course it didn't count! I wore jeans and a sweater and the pancakes were a last minute idea for two hungry people needing to break up a long commute. It definitely didn't count... *did it?* I brushed the question away, firmly stuffing it into the back of my mind. *This* was a date. I'd been to Francine's many times over the years but never out on a dinner date, although I wanted to, and it didn't disappoint.

The lights were dimmed, and each table had flickering candles inside miniature hurricane lanterns in the middle of the checkered tablecloths. Soft music played through speakers that were discreetly placed around the room. The tables were already half full with pairs of customers seeking intimate dinners. I nodded and said hello to several patrons I recognized as we passed them on the way to our table. I was sure half the town would know about my date by tomorrow.

"I mean it," said Tom, his voice full of effortless charm. "You are the most beautiful woman in Calendar."

"How many women have you seen since you got here?" I asked, narrowing my eyes in mock suspicion of his effortless charm.

"Including tonight?" I nodded and he held up his hands, counting on his fingers. "Let's see. A dozen?"

I laughed.

"You mean there's more?" Tom opened his mouth wider, pretending to look shocked. "So what's good on the menu?"

"I've heard everything is good," I told him.

"This isn't your regular date joint?"

"I don't have a regular date anything," I admitted, feeling a little embarrassed. "I've been single for a while."

"Me too. My last girlfriend dumped me with a text."

"Ouch!"

"It wasn't even a text to me!" he admitted. "But something that was passed along."

I winced. "Double ouch." I thought about it a moment, and before I wavered, I said, "I caught my ex making out with his 'supposed' best friend."

"Ouch!"

"On my mom's couch."

"At least he wasn't making out *with* your mom," said Tom. He caught my eye and we burst into laughter at the absurdity of that, pushing the painful memory aside. It was a horrible moment for me and laughing about it now made me suddenly feel that I finally healed from it. I felt lighter and brighter. My ex was no more than a bad memory now, and that made me smile.

"Here's to new beginnings," said Tom, raising his glass after we perused the wine menu. He insisted on ordering a bottle of white with an unpronounceable name.

"New beginnings," I agreed, clinking my glass against his. I sipped the wine, enjoying the delicious flavor.

"And to not dropping anymore gloves," added Tom, raising his glass again.

"I'm with you there," I laughed. "Where would I be if you hadn't returned my glove?"

"Home alone? Battling through a harsh winter with one very cold hand?" suggested Tom. "I am so glad I caught up with you, not only to return it. If you don't mind me asking, what were you doing at the police station? Nothing wrong, I hope?"

"I wasn't being arrested if that's what you're implying!" I gasped, halfway horrified that he would think that, and halfway amused that he could.

"No, you don't look like a jailbird! You're far too glamorous."

My cheeks flushed but I wasn't sure if it was the wine or the steady stream of compliments. "No one has ever called me *glamorous* before."

Tom gave me a skeptical look. "I find that hard to believe. Since we've established you're not a jailbird, I'm going to make a guess. You're—" He paused, tapping his forefinger against his chin "—an undercover detective?"

"Guess again."

"Traffic cop?"

"Nope."

"Something to do with the law?"

I shook my head. "I'm a librarian."

"Very interesting. Let's see. Since you weren't being arrested for a crime, you must have been there to report one. Hmm, now I'm wondering what kind of crimes are committed here. Did someone drop too much litter?"

I held back a giggle. "No."

"Paint their house the wrong color?"

"No!"

"Forget to clean their car last Sunday?"

"That's not even a law!"

"It isn't?" Tom laughed again. "Okay, you got me, I give up."

"Actually, my friend, Bree, was killed," I said, growing somber. "That is, she was a colleague but I considered her my friend. I thought I knew her pretty well, but now I'm not sure I did. I really liked her though." I trailed off, aware I was rambling.

Tom reached for my hand and gave it a gentle squeeze as he wrapped his fingers around mine. "I feel I should apologize for being so flippant. I made a dumb joke when you're obviously dealing with something horrible. Were you helping the police?"

"It was just an interview. Standard stuff, I suppose."

"I really don't know police procedure but, from what I've seen on TV, I assume they must interview a lot of people."

"I think I know about as much as you do about procedure. I'm just trying to help in any way I can."

"I'm sure they appreciate it too. You could probably tell the police a lot about your friend."

"I thought I could too but when Detective Logan asked me questions, I realized I didn't know anything about Bree and what I thought I knew turned out not to be true."

"Are you sure someone killed her? Could she have possibly taken her own life?"

"Detective Logan says someone killed her. I found her body; and unfortunately, it looks like he's right."

"You must have been terrified."

I relished the comforting warmth of Tom's hand, fully aware he hadn't let go in all the time we'd been talking. "I was. I've never found a dead body before."

"Does the detective... Logan, wasn't that his name? Does Detective Logan know who did it?"

I shook my head. "No, he's just as mystified as I am."

"No leads at all? Surely someone must have seen something?"

"It was a horrible night. Dark and snowing. No one was around. I'm afraid whoever killed her might get away with it," I said, realizing that thought had plagued me all day.

"I hope you feel safe here with me. I'll even walk you to your door tonight and if you need me to check out all your closets and windows, I promise I will."

A little sigh over his unbridled chivalry escaped me. "That's very kind of you."

"Do you want to talk anymore about it?"

"No, but thank you. I'm trying not to think about it. It's too awful. Why don't you tell me more about you? What brings you to Calendar?"

"Funny story," started Tom, launching into a tale of a business venture that was proving anything but easy. In no time at all, I was laughing and gasping, pushing all the morbid thoughts of Bree aside, and the guilty twinges of being able to enjoy myself lessened substantially when we ordered our appetizers before moving on to our entrees. The delectable aromas enticed me, along with the food warming my belly and the wine running through my veins. By the time we reached dessert—Tom offered to split a chocolate souffle after I protested that I couldn't eat another bite—I was ready to declare our date the best I ever had. Of course, I would never admit that to him, or that he had little competition. Except... Jason was such wonderful company throughout the day too. He rescued me when I blew a tire although he could have left me at the side of the road. He also drove me all the way to the city and back without a single complaint. We strolled around the public library and he was so charming that I was still thinking about him now, even while on a date with another man! I could not think about Jason right now!

"I would suggest we take a walk but I think the rain might change our minds," said Tom, pulling me back to the moment. He nodded towards the windows facing the street. I turned, only then realizing we were the last diners in the restaurant. How could it have emptied without me ever noticing?

"I wish you saw Calendar when it was prettier, not like this. The snow was lovely until all the recent rain washed it mostly away. It's stunningly beautiful in the summer."

"I'm sure I can come back and visit," said Tom, raising his hand to signal the server for the check. He declined my offer to split the cost, emphatically refusing when I offered more than once. He paid and a moment later, the same server returned with our coats. "I'm parked outside. May I offer you a lift?" asked Tom.

"Please," I said. "I don't live too far."

At my house, he idled the car before shutting off the engine and getting out before walking around to my side. When I stepped out, an umbrella appeared above my head. "Where did that come from?" I asked.

"Magic." Tom winked. He held it over both of us as we walked to my door. At the stoop, he lingered. "I meant it when I offered to check your closets. And just so you know, I'm not trying to get an invitation inside, I just want you to feel safe."

"I'm sure I am safe," I told him. "I have a good alarm system but I really appreciate your offer."

"Why don't I call you tomorrow morning? For my own peace of mind."

"That would be nice, thank you."

"I'm not being entirely altruistic. I'd like to see you again and I think you mentioned something about a tour of the town?"

"I'd be happy to give you a tour if you're not busy."

"I'll make sure I'm not."

"Good night, Tom."

Tom leaned over, and for a moment, I thought he would kiss me but he dipped his head to one side, brushing his lips against my cheek. "Good night, Sara."

I let myself inside, waggling my fingers in a wave as Tom turned and walked back along the path. At the end of it, he slipped on the slick sidewalk, and a leg flew out to his left, while an arm flailed off to the right, yet somehow, he managed to keep his umbrella aloft. When he righted himself, he turned around, laughing, and bowed. I was still chuckling as I shut the door and slipped off my shoes. I entered the code into the alarm keypad, switched on the lights and closed the curtains before going into the kitchen to get a glass of water. As I returned to the living room, a knock sounded at the door. Tom must have forgotten something. *Was it a goodnight kiss?* Although the cheek kiss was gentlemanly, it didn't exactly buckle my knees.

I opened the door but instead of Tom, the porch light illuminated another man.

"Detective Logan!" I exclaimed, my heart sinking. He could only have come here so late if there were bad news to report. "Has something happened?"

"May I come in?"

I opened the door a little wider, stepping back to allow him to pass. "This is very late for a social call," I said as he shrugged off his jacket, hanging it on my coat rack rather than allowing it to drip across the living room.

"I tried to come by earlier but you weren't home. I saw your lights on and I wanted to share some news about Bree," he said simply.

"Oh?" I waved Detective Logan over to the couch and he perched on the edge while I sat adjacent to him, waiting for what he had to say. Did he somehow hear about my trip to the city? I braced myself, anticipating a scolding lecture.

"I shouldn't be sharing this with you but you're the only person I know who spent any real time with Bree," he said as he reached into his pocket for a sheaf of folded paper. I took it from him, speed reading it as my jaw dropped.

I stared hard at the rap sheet, my mind full of questions. Yet, all I could stammer was, "How? How could this be possible?"

"You tell me," said Detective Logan.

With his face no more revealing than a mask, I wasn't sure how Logan felt about the latest developments in Bree's case, but I was horrified. So much for my theory about her being on the run from an ex or having correctly deduced the identities of the criminals responsible for the heists. Bree really was on the run from the law.

"I can't picture Bree as a criminal, not at all," I said finally.

"All the evidence is there, Sara. I checked and double-checked her prints. I called each police department that has any connection to her, be it solid or slight, and they all told me the same thing. She's not just any old, smash-and-grab thief."

"Smash-and-grab?" I repeated, looking up at the detective.

"The type that runs in and grabs something before smashing their way out. This woman was a sophisticated professional. She cased her targets in advance, developed a plan, and walked out with whatever she set her eyes on. Art, antiques, and in the latest case, diamonds. They think she might have gotten set up to take the fall on the last heist, which could have been why she went underground."

"Do you think she came here just to hide?" I asked, again recalling the conversation Meredith overheard.

"I think that's exactly what she did."

"But why? Surely she must have sold whatever she stole? She probably already had a fence lined up, or maybe she even stole particular things per order. No thief would keep such high value items for too long. It would be way too risky."

"Sounds like you know what you're talking about?"

I shook my head. "Not exactly. We had an engaging author who spoke at the library last year. He was fascinating. His hero, or anti-hero, I guess, was an art thief that specialized in high-end robberies, you know, kind of making the impossible heist possible. He described it so interestingly and made it sound so real."

"I'm sure he did but this is real life. We've got a real problem here. The last robbery victimized an established jeweler and it amounts to more than one hundred carats of diamonds, including a very rare, yellow diamond, amongst other precious gems."

I couldn't help the gasp that escaped me. My head whirred until it clicked on what Detective Logan meant. "There's only one reason why someone would kill her," I said, thinking carefully. "She must have had something they wanted but was it cash or jewels or something else?"

"I'm putting my money on the jewels."

"The money I found in her apartment isn't enough if she sold them, is it?"

"Not even close. We're talking somewhere in the millions, not the thousands."

I thought about the other articles I found in the box. They were still stuffed in my jacket pocket where I shoved them earlier. "If I tell you something, please don't get mad." I looked up, attempting to implore Detective Logan with my eyes.

"Spit it out, Sara," he said.

"I went to her apartment..." I started.

"You did what?" Detective Logan yelled. "Didn't I warn you repeatedly about staying away from her apartment?"

"No, not that one! Her other apartment, the one in the city. The address registered on the driver's license I gave you."

"You went there? Are you crazy? You had no idea what you could be walking into!"

"I know that now!"

"Tell me you took someone with you at least."

I winced. "No, I got a lift."

Detective Logan let out a long sigh and ran his hand over his auburn hair. "What did you learn?"

"Nothing much. I met her roommate. She was annoyed that Bree, or *Brittany*, as she knew her, disappeared although she wasn't too concerned. She said she was glad Bree and her creepy friends weren't hanging around anymore. She thought Bree had a boyfriend called Tricky."

"Tricky?"

"That's what she said. Does that help at all?"

"I'll run the name against any known associates but I'm not holding out much hope."

"There's something else," I told him as I got up, crossing over to the coat rack. I pulled the articles from my coat pocket and held them out. Logan took them, shuffling through in the time it took to read the headlines. "These were in a box her roommate gave me. She asked me to give it to Bree. I implied we were related. Do you think these were the heists Bree could have been involved in?"

"Possibly. Or maybe she was studying them. I'll look into them a bit more. What else was in the box?"

"Nothing. Just random stuff. I'm sorry, Detective, I left it there."

"I'll get someone to pick it up and interview the roommate on record. Can you promise me something?"

"What?"

"Swear to me you won't go back there! Bree was probably involved with some bad people and I think one of them killed her. If millions were at stake, they wouldn't hesitate to hurt anyone who got in their way."

"Do you think Bree still has the diamonds?" Logan had me worried now. If the mystery man discovered me in the apartment while I was hidden in the bed frame, things could have gone very badly. I couldn't help thinking about the poor jewelry store manager and his family. Theft! Kidnapping! Murder! Bree's associates were definitely bad news.

"I do and I think that's why she came to our quiet, little town. She wanted to lie low until she could pick them up from wherever she hid them and sell them. Someone else just figured out her plan and killed her. I have no doubt they are looking for whatever she hid and if it is jewels, they're worth a helluva lot. I'm only telling you that because I want you to understand how serious it is."

"I appreciate you doing so," I told him as he got onto his feet, moving towards the door.

"Bree got herself mixed up in some nasty business. She either double-crossed the wrong person or maybe they never intended for her to get her cut. Either way, she's paid the ultimate price now and I have to make sure no one else gets harmed."

"I get the message," I told him. "Stay away from Bree's apartments. Be on the lookout for anyone asking about diamonds."

Detective Logan laughed, his face lighting up pleasantly. Now, I realized he could be good looking when he wasn't so dour. "I don't think they'll be that obvious. Call me if you feel suspicious about anything. Anything at all."

"I will," I assured him.

Detective Logan paused in the doorway to zip his jacket. "I do have one good piece of news," he said.

"Oh?"

"You can officially go back to the library now."

"Really?" I smiled, my mood instantly lifting. "Thank you so much!"

I shut the door behind him, waiting until he reached his car before I switched off the porch light. I wouldn't admit it to him but his news worried me. Bree took something very valuable and whoever wanted it would clearly stop at nothing to get it back.

CHAPTER FOURTEEN

"Sara! Yoo-hoo! Sara!"

I turned around, searching out the voice and spotted Candice at the door of the café, waving hard. I waved back and crossed the road, allowing her to usher me inside and into a chair where Jaclyn and my mother waited.

"Have you heard?" asked Candice.

"Heard what?" I replied, looking at each of the expectant faces.

Candice leaned in. "Bree was a jewel thief," she said in a low voice. "She stole millions of dollars worth of jewels."

"How do you know that?" I asked, wondering why the news surprised me so much. The Calendar gossip mill must have launched into the emergency news phone tree overnight. I would have been surprised if anyone in town didn't know by now. This had to be the juiciest news the town ever heard.

"My sister, Tamsin, told me and she heard it from her friend, Jessica, whose cousin is married to Danielle, who knows Joe Nixon, down at the police station," said Jaclyn. Her leg was propped up on another chair and she did her best to look comfortable. I figured she was desperate to return behind the counter but until her leg healed, holding court here was the best she could do.

"Oh," I cooed, amazed that the news had traveled so far and remained intact.

"But you can't tell anyone," said Jaclyn. "I don't want anyone to get into any trouble."

"I won't tell anyone."

"Me either," chorused the other ladies.

"I already heard it from my neighbor, Alice, who heard it from her son who lives next to Sam Logan's father," said my mother. She looked very satisfied. "So I think it's safe to say the secret is out."

"Detective Logan is not going to be happy that everyone knows his business," I said, receiving a collective shake of heads and some worried murmurs.

"So it's true?" asked Candice.

"Huh?"

"When Mrs. Stanley came in her for morning latte, she said Detective Logan was at your house last night; since he didn't arrest you, we figured it was because he came to tell you something," said Candice.

"He told me I could open the library now," I said, glossing over the details that the ladies might have found more interesting. The town might know the headline news but they definitely didn't need to hear the rest of the details from me! Plus, the last thing I needed to incur was Detective Logan's wrath. I'd been lucky enough last night. I didn't need to push him any further.

"That's great news!" said my mother, reaching for my hand and giving me a happy squeeze.

"It is, isn't it? I don't have a lot of time left in my campaign to keep it open so I thought I should get started right away with an upcoming event to prove just how much the library is loved. Can I count on all of you to come?" I asked. The idea popped into my head when I awoke and I relished the convenient distraction.

"Absolutely. I'll bake something and turn it into a real party," said Candice.

"I could bring some of my homemade wine," said Mom. "And the coffee and tea urns we use for big gatherings."

"And I'll bring tiny cups for the wine so no one blows their mind. That stuff can be lethal!" added Jaclyn.

I laughed. "It all sounds wonderful. I'll make up some flyers and put them around town. Tell as many people as you can."

"Speaking of telling people things, why don't you tell us all about your date with that handsome, young man last night?" said Mom. "It sounded like you two were very romantic."

I blushed and giggled. "Does everyone know?" They nodded. "I thought so. Tom and I had a lovely time, thank you. We ate dinner, drank a little wine, and he drove me home. He was the perfect gentleman the whole time."

"So when is date number two?" asked Jaclyn, glancing toward my mother who was waiting just as eagerly.

I was about to tell her I wasn't sure when the café door banged open. My friend Rachel, rushed inside, and a blast of cold air followed her. She looked around, saw me, and hurried over, throwing her arms around me before greeting everyone else. "I just heard about Bree!" she exclaimed. "How awful to discover that you were harboring a criminal!"

"I wasn't harboring..."

She cut me off, "You must be terrified. You never can tell, can you? Bree looked so innocent but underneath it all, something dark was lurking."

"I really don't think anything was lurk..."

"I wonder if she was casing the whole town?"

"Why? There's nothing to steal," said my mother. "I think she hid her loot here until the police stopped looking for her. Then she planned to dig it up and take off."

"Where do you think she hid it?" asked Rachel. She pulled off her hat, releasing a tumble of long blonde hair and undid the buttons of her coat as she waited.

I tuned the gossip out as I drank the coffee Candice placed in front of me, thinking about the library. It would be so strange to open it up again, especially knowing that Bree died there only days before. Despite my doubts over many of the things I thought I knew about her, I was sure her love for the library was real. Perhaps it was silly of me to assume, but I truly believed Bree wanted me to save the library. I pushed away the annoying, little voice that told me she didn't care at all, and simply wanted to hide out in my sleepy, little town until it was safe for her to disappear forever.

Taking a deep breath, I remembered Bree suggested a number of ideas for library events and also spent many enthusiastic hours helping to plan them. Unless she were a brilliantly accomplished actress, she couldn't have done that without some kind of genuine interest.

There was another thing that worried me. It seemed so frivolous to hold an event where Bree had died only days before, but if I didn't start campaigning, there was no hope for the library's preservation. It didn't seem like I had any other choice. I had to do it.

"What do you think, Sara?" asked my mother.

"Hmm?" I frowned and blinked, wondering what I missed.

"I asked if you knew when Bree's family were coming to town?"

"Oh, I don't know. I doubt she had any," I said.

"That is so sad. Who's going to bury her?"

That problem never occurred to me. "I don't know," I told them. Bree was my friend, regardless of everything else. I felt that strongly about her. I couldn't subject her to the mercy of some bureaucratic decision. "I guess if no one shows up, I will," I decided.

"You have a kind heart, Sara. I hope someone shows up at her funeral, even if she were bad news," said Jaclyn. "You've raised a good daughter, Nadine."

"Maybe some of her criminal pals will come," said Mom and the gossip started all over again.

Gathering my coat and purse, I slipped away from the table unnoticed.

"They just don't stop, do they?" said Candice from behind the counter.

"They will talk about this for weeks," I agreed, watching my mother and Jaclyn as they drew Rachel into their conversation.

"Is there any truth to what they're saying?"

"Some, but I think that will be diluted soon enough."

"I know it doesn't mean much, but I really liked Bree. I'm sorry she died in such a horrible way and I hope whoever did it is brought to justice, and fast." Candice busied herself arranging baked goods under the glass cloches that sat on the counter.

"Me too. I must go and get those flyers printed. See you later?"

"You can count on it. I won't bake a cake because I prefer to make lots of bite-sized favorites. You know, brownies, cupcakes, cookies. I just watched a tutorial on how to make edible wafers that look exactly like book covers."

"They sound amazing but please don't spend all your time on this. I can't pay you much. The library's budget is very constrained."

"Consider it my contribution to the Save the Library campaign and also a little marketing ploy for me when I open that bakery one day. It's my pleasure, really, Sara. I'll enjoy it."

I thanked Candice, pleased with her efforts and suggestions, and stepped outside, buoyed by her support. I raised my hand to wave to Detective Logan as he drove past in his police car but I saw his heavy frown and he didn't seem to notice me. I felt sorry for him. He was going to have a hell of a time trying to calm the town gossip. In a couple of hours, he would probably be inundated with people who "might have" seen something or "possibly" heard something. In reality, they would all be angling for some new information to astonish their friends.

I tucked my chin into my jacket and hurried to the small print shop further down the street, glad for a reprieve from the nearly relentless rain. If it rained later, it would definitely impede the turnout for my impromptu event. It was bad enough that Calendar was enduring a sustained cold snap, but the now incessant rain managed to drag everyone's mood down. I couldn't wait until spring arrived, so the trees could grow leaves and the flowers could bloom in the gardens. And the sad business about Bree would have already been resolved.

The possibility that the library wouldn't exist then pinched my heart. I loved working there and even though I was sure I would still have a job at the new library in the building Jason's firm delegated as "suitable," it simply wouldn't be the same. Perhaps I should do what Bree did: try something entirely new.

I laughed aloud, surprising a woman who was walking a tiny, fluffy dog dressed in its own yellow, hooded, rain jacket. Changing jobs was practical but comparing myself to Bree definitely wasn't. For all the qualities I liked in her, I had to remind myself that she was a fugitive and a criminal. She didn't just change jobs. She took off with millions and selected my town to hide in under an assumed name and job she gained purely by subterfuge.

The print shop, combined with a stationer's, also carried a wide range of newspapers and magazines. It was empty when I stepped inside. I pulled the flyer from my bag and peeled back the protective, plastic cover, setting it on top of the large printer.

"Good morning," called a cheerful voice. "Oh, it's you, Sara. I just saw your mother over at the café. How are you?"

"Very well, thank you. I came in to print these," I said, holding up my flyer as Antonio, the shop's proprietor, ambled over. "They're for an event occurring at the library tonight."

"It's open now? I heard about what happened. Such a terrible thing to befall a poor, young girl. Did they catch whomever did it?"

"Not yet, but I'm sure Detective Logan will."

"Bet he didn't think he'd ever have to solve a murder in Calendar."

"I doubt anyone thought that," I agreed.

"True. How many copies do you need?"

"Fifty, I think. I want to make sure I can leave one in every shop, café, and noticeboard."

"Why don't you print some extras? I can ask my niece, Addison, to put them in the mailboxes when she takes my special offer pamphlet out to distribute. A lot more people will see the flyers that way."

"That would be great!"

"Print whatever you need and leave me a copy. I'll print the rest and give them to Addison when she finishes school."

I pulled a ten-dollar bill from my purse and offered it to Antonio but he waved it away, saying, "Consider it my contribution for the campaign to preserve the library. I can't believe our council would tear it down just so that bigshot developer can put a bunch of tract houses on the land. I gave him a piece of my mind already!"

"Really?"

"Absolutely. I saw him outside the library this morning."

I stopped, my hand gripping the lid. "What was he doing there?" I asked.

"I have no idea. I was outside walking Mindy and I saw him strolling around like he owned the place."

"Huh." I closed the lid and hit the print button.

"After I told him what I thought of big firms like his trying to bulldoze little towns like ours and make them all look the same, he said he'd take my opinion to the board, and then he walked off into the gardens."

"The library gardens?"

"Yes. What do you think he was doing there? Looking for Bree's hidden treasure?"

I should have guessed the conversation would come around to that. "You heard about that?"

Antonio huffed. "Who hasn't? My wife woke me up to tell me and you won't believe who she heard it from!"

I hit the print button again, only half listening as the machine began to shoot out more copies of my flyer. I couldn't imagine what Jason needed in the library gardens but Antonio's comment bothered me. If he thought Bree might have hidden her treasure in the garden, then other people might think that too. What if Jason went there to look for them?

What if other people decided the library gardens contained millions in treasure just waiting to be found? I usually left the gates open so that people could stroll in whenever they liked but perhaps it would be more sensible to lock them now. If only to discourage anyone from amateur treasure hunting. I decided to do just that just as soon as I finished distributing all the flyers.

I left Antonio with a flyer as requested and stepped outside, slipping in a puddle that collected outside the door. Just as I began to slide, my arms flailing, the flyers flapping, a pair of strong arms caught me.

"I've got you."

"Tom! Thank you so much." I looked around, noticing one sheet had slipped from my grip, landing face up in the puddle.

"What's this?" he asked, stooping to pluck the wet page from the pavement.

"It's a flyer for an event I'm hosting at the library tonight. I have to distribute them all around town."

"What's happening to the library?" he asked, reading.

"It's in imminent danger of being shut down," I said, quickly filling him in on the difficulties the library faced. "So, you see, I don't want to seem unsympathetic to what happened to Bree but we're running out of time."

"Let me help you," he said, reaching for the flyers. "Two people can do this a lot faster than one, which will leave you with some free time."

"For what?" I wondered.

"To have lunch with me." Tom smiled and I couldn't help smiling back. "You can tell me all about this little town of yours and whether or not all the gossip about hidden treasure is true."

I sighed. "You've heard the gossip as well?"

"Guess so. The proprietor of my hotel spoke of nothing else and I think it's fascinating. Hey, here's an idea. You knew your friend better than anyone else.

Why don't you find the jewels and use the money to save the library? You could even buy it to make sure it never gets knocked down!"

"If there are any jewels, they're stolen property. They wouldn't be mine to keep but I like your way of thinking."

"Maybe there's a healthy finder's fee?" Tom widened his eyes and raised his eyebrows, making me laugh with his infectious enthusiasm.

"Let's try my way to save the library first," I told him as I hooked my arm through his when he offered it. "And leave the jewels for the police to find."

"That doesn't sound like much fun but I'll indulge you. Lead the way."

CHAPTER FIFTEEN

After Tom and I parted ways—with the firm assurance that he was looking forward to attending the event—I headed over to the library. Choosing the shorter route, the one that took me past Bree's apartment on Oak Street, I was hoping that the route itself didn't violate Detective Logan's warning to stay away.

If someone in a police car were watching her house, it wasn't a marked car, and I thought I recognized one of the junior officers parked in his truck. Waving to him, I walked over and he cranked down the window as I approached.

"Hi, Joe, or should I say, Officer Nixon," I said, handing him one of my flyers. "If you can manage to get off work in time, please come to this event later."

"How do you know I'm working?" he asked, frowning as he scanned the flyer.

I glanced over my shoulder, instantly confirming my initial suspicion. "Because sitting here, I doubt if you just *happen to have* the perfect view of Bree's door. Any luck?"

"None," he replied, looking chagrined at being spotted so easily. "Logan told me surveillance would be boring but I never imagined it would be *this* dull. Plus, I'm freezing my ass off waiting for something to happen."

"I read in a book that city cops who are assigned to doing this kind of thing often bring their own blankets just to keep warm," I told him.

"I'll try to remember that if I ever have to do it again! I don't suppose Logan will mind if I tell you something, since you already heard the man breaking in, but I sincerely doubt any bad guys are going to show up. Certainly not with all the treasure hunters stopping by the apartment every ten minutes."

"Treasure hunters?"

"You haven't heard about what your friend stole?"

"Of course I have!" I replied, wondering exactly how far the gossip had spread, not to mention, how corrupted it now must have become.

"Folks figure them jewels have got to be around here somewhere. Someone dug up most of the yard last night and I already chased some kids off for raiding the flower planters next to her steps."

"That isn't even Bree's yard! It belongs to Mrs. Kowalski who lives in the first floor apartment!"

"I know. She already filed a report about it." Joe raised his chin, indicating I should look behind me. I turned to see Mrs. Kowalski shuffling around in her yard, a small spade in one hand. "I think she decided to

167

check it out for herself. She makes a good guard dog, if you'll pardon the expression."

I watched Mrs. Kowalski digging a hole next to a green bush. "Do people really think Bree buried the jewels somewhere in Calendar?" I asked, turning back.

"They haven't been found yet, so they have to be somewhere," Joe reasoned.

"It would be nice if someone put more effort into tracking down the fiend that killed Bree rather than what they might find in someone's backyard."

"Money always brings out the worst in people."

I commiserated again over him being saddled with the unenviable job of watching over the house. Privately, I agreed with him. It seemed highly unlikely that the man I overheard would return. If he were watching the apartment inconspicuously, he surely would have witnessed the officer's presence, Mrs. Kowalski and countless others in the vicinity. When I thought more about it, I decided it was also unlikely that Bree would have buried a valuable haul nearby. She always struck me as being quite smart. If she did hide the jewels, it would have been smarter to stash them somewhere easily accessible but not too closeby. The jewels might not even be in Calendar! Bree could have hidden them somewhere along the way, long before she even arrived here.

As I said goodbye and stepped away, I heard a commotion behind me. I stopped and watched Joe get out of the truck and jog across the road. A moment later, he was chasing a pair of teenagers from the garden while Mrs. Kowalski followed close behind, waving her hand spade angrily and shouting at the audacious trespassers. I shook my head and continued my journey, wondering what I should say to Jason when I reached the library.

A few minutes later, without deciding on anything to say if he were still there, I reached the library's iron garden gate. I opened it and stepped through, but a shiver vibrated down my spine. It wasn't just the cold, although the bitter morning was quite chilly, but something else. I paused, listening closely, and trying to work out what could have alerted my senses.

From behind the library, I heard a faint voice! No. There were two voices.

Latching the gate to the post to keep it open, I stepped into the garden, and began following the path as it curved around the library. My nerves were jangled. When I decided to become a librarian, I envisaged a cozy life of handling rare, old books, devouring catalogues, and encouraging children to build a lifetime of dreams and adventures from their own homes. I didn't anticipate creeping around library gardens, with my heels crunching on the gravel, or searching for people who didn't belong there. In the middle of winter, absolutely no one belonged in the garden! Sure, it was often open for public access on most days, but few people opted to walk in the garden during the snowy or wet months.

When I found the source of the voices, I stopped in a dead halt. "What's going on?" I asked, taking in the strange sight. If I hadn't just heard Joe's description of the people he saw around Bree's apartment, I would have been less prepared than I was now. Even so, I looked at the hand trowels in the Rileys' hands with utter disbelief. Still worse, several large holes had already been dug around the evergreen bushes and the majestic, old oak tree.

"We didn't do that," said Mr. Riley. Both he and his wife were prominent members of the gardening club, whose meetings my mother occasionally attended. However, I was willing to bet a large sum of money that this activity had nothing to do with that.

"Uh-huh," I replied, knowing my face could not mask my suspicion.

"We really didn't. It was like this when we got here!"

"See?" said Mrs. Riley, holding up her hand trowel. It looked like it had never been used, but maybe she could have cleaned it. Perhaps they really didn't dig the holes, but it surely appeared they had come here armed to do so. Someone had simply beaten them to it.

"Anyone else in here?" I asked.

"No, just us."

"We thought the garden looked a little overgrown so we came to do the maintenance and found it exactly like this," said Mr. Riley, persisting with his transparent ruse.

"And this gardening maintenance has nothing to do with that silly rumor that millions of dollars in jewels were buried somewhere in Calendar?" I sighed, knowing that no matter what they said, it wouldn't be the truth.

"What?" gasped Mr. Riley.

"No!" exclaimed his wife.

"Surely not!"

"Our civic duty..."

Their excuses came thick and fast.

"Nothing is buried here," I assured them, pointing to the holes, "and if there were, someone already beat you to it. I'll escort you out now and let's not worry about the gardening. The town council sends a regular gardener to do the maintenance once-a-month. Let's go." I hurried the couple out of the garden, shaking my head at their continued protests of charitable intentions. When I'd seen them out of the gates, I unlocked the rarely used padlock and secured it through the notch. It might not put off any serious attempts to dig up the garden but could deter anyone who was unable to scale the gate and the fence.

I was surprised to find the Rileys there, having expected to see Jason. If he were the one behind the huge holes, he would definitely get a piece of my mind! Despite how hard I tried, I just couldn't picture him digging up the garden in search of mystery treasure. Not that I didn't think he had the strength—he definitely did —but I couldn't see him excavating any dirt without a plan or some real indication of where the treasure might be buried. The holes were haphazardly scooped out rather than being dug with any serious intention. However, since Jason wasn't around, I couldn't ask him.

Walking around to the front of the building, I pulled out my phone. Jason gave me his phone number on the way to the city if I needed to call him. I hadn't planned on using his number again, but now I had to. Standing in the doorway, my thumb hovering over his name, I was hesitating. Only when a shadow fell over the phone, did I realize I didn't need to call him.

"Hi," said Jason, looking pleased to see me.

I dropped my phone into my pocket. "I was just going to call you," I told him.

A smile spread across his face. "That would have been a nice surprise."

"Would it?" I asked, unable to keep the note of annoyance from my voice. "I heard you were in the library garden earlier and I just found it all dug up."

"Dug up?" Jason frowned.

I glanced at his hands, noticing the lack of any spade or signs of dirt. Not that it mattered. He could have easily stowed a shovel in his car and wiped off the loose dirt. I looked down for more evidence of digging but noted the hem of his slacks looked neat and clean and his polished shoes didn't show any traces of dirt.

Sighing, I felt more relieved than disappointed. Jason couldn't possibly be a treasure hunter. "Some people are convinced that Bree buried her loot somewhere in town. I just chased a couple of people armed with hand spades from the garden and had to lock the gate. Don't laugh!" I warned, seeing him struggle to hold it in. He gave up and burst out laughing and within seconds, I joined him. "I think the town has gone crazy," I continued. "One whiff of millions and everyone is looking for X marks the spot! Even Bree's ancient, downstairs neighbor is outside digging in her garden and the police said someone dug up the plant pots near her door."

"I barely knew Bree but I don't think she would bury something that precious in a plant pot. And yes," he added, "I heard all the rumors about the treasure. All the employees of the Maple Tree Hotel talked about nothing else this morning."

"That's what I thought. And you know what? I don't even know that I care where the jewels are… unless they're the key to finding her killer."

The amused look on Jason's face vanished. "You still think someone is hanging around to get them?"

"I don't know. Maybe."

"Then the safest thing to do is stay as far away as possible."

I nodded, without making any commitment to do that. It was true that I didn't care about the jewels, although Tom's suggestion that a finder's fee could possibly save the library was more than a little enticing. What did interest me was that Bree's killer and the other thief, the one Bree might have double-crossed, could be the same person. If that person were willing to take her life in exchange for the jewels' location, surely if they had that information they would have already been long gone? The more I thought about what I overheard from the man's one-sided conversation in her apartment, the more I believed she refused to confess her secret. Another thought struck me: he was speaking to someone on the other end. So there was definitely more than one person involved.

"What are you doing here anyway?" I asked, remembering why I'd been looking for him.

"My firm asked me to take some measurements."

"Is that why you were in the garden earlier? Someone saw you and mentioned it to me."

"So you checked to make sure I'm not digging it up? I'm not, Sara, I swear! I had to take new measurements of the building."

My mood dropped. "Don't you already have everything you need for the purchase?"

"My firm does."

"Then I think your work here is done," I replied tartly, reaching for my keys.

"Wait. Are you opening up?"

"Sorry to disappoint you, but yes," I snapped. "Detective Logan cleared the library and told me to go ahead and open up as normal."

"Oh. That's good news."

I blinked back my surprise. I fully expected Jason to be disappointed or even scathing at the reopening of the library, especially now, with little more than a couple of weeks to save it. Perhaps he simply decided there was no point rubbing it in any longer, not when he assumed nothing more could be done. I wasn't sure if it were kindness, which would have been endearing, or the satisfaction of knowing his firm was getting away with destroying the beautiful, old building.

"It must be cold inside," he continued, surprising me again.

"I expect so. I'm sure I'll warm up as soon as I get things organized. I plan on reopening tomorrow." I started to tell him about the party but thought better of it. Inviting Jason was like asking him to watch us fail. Determined as I was, I knew it would take a miracle to win this fight. Perhaps Tom's idea to find the jewels first wasn't a bad suggestion!

"Why don't I bring you a coffee?"

"I..." I started, unsure of what to say. I'd been so determined to be pithy and sharp that his offer made me forget all about that.

"I'll be back soon," he said, waving as he took the path before I could protest.

I wasn't sure how I felt about Jason's company but I unlocked the doors, stepping inside the empty building. I reached for the wall panel, flicking on every light, illuminating the dark interior, and pushed the door shut behind me, nudging it with my shoulder when it stuck. Waiting in the entryway, I shivered, suddenly feeling very uncertain. Normally, the library was a place I relished. Being alone in the midst of the old books, breathing in the mixed scent of leather and paper, and observing the patterns of dappled light from the stained-glass window on the stairs always seemed such a luxury, but today it felt unnatural and different. Someone had died here only days before. Someone had taken her last breath in there, just like the library would soon. The juxtaposition of the two awful events made my jaw tremble and I pressed my hand to my mouth, holding back the sob that was climbing up my throat.

I sucked in a long breath and blew it out, forcing myself to repeat the action until my breathing was steady and calm.

"C'mon, Sara," I pep-talked, cramming all my reserves of energy into my speech. "You can either stand in the doorway, without turning around, and never come back; or you can get to work and start making this place party-ready. If not for you, then do it for Bree and the whole town; they deserve to keep this library." The words I rattled in my head revived me. I unzipped my jacket but decided not to take it off until the generator had pumped some heat into the building. Lifting one foot forward, then the next, I walked deeper into the library, gaining more purpose with each step.

Starting at the desk that served as the command center, I scooped up all the books. They had been lying there since the doors were last closed. I carefully loaded them onto the trolley. Next, I sat at the desk and sorted through the small stack of mail. I busied myself organizing, sorting and shuffling the desk items until eventually, there was nothing left for me to do.

The only thing that could combat the chill was exercise. I pushed the chair under the desk and reached for the trolley, pushing it along and returning the various books to their proper shelves. Taking my time to neaten the racks, I also ensured the displays were rotated. By the time I returned the trolley to the desk, I had come to a grim conclusion.

I was avoiding the upper floor.

At some point, I had to go upstairs. With a rush, I realized how well I avoided even thinking about taking the stairs to the upper floor. I had to. I couldn't postpone it forever, yet I wasn't sure if I were ready for whatever I might find up there.

After another restoring deep breath, I propelled myself forwards, walking quickly before I changed my mind. I took the stairs without pausing to smile at the stained-glass beam that I usually found so pleasing. Instead, I pushed onwards.

I wasn't sure what I expected to find now the police had released the scene. Previously there hadn't been the faint chalk outline of a body or some leftover crime scene tape. What did I imagine now? Bree's ghost! But there was nothing left to mark the crime.

Moving around, I stopped when I saw the dark stain, no more than a foot across, that I'd seen the last time I entered. It was so dark, it almost disappeared against the dark wooden floors but I could still see it.

I turned away quickly, unable to look at it any longer and marched over to the display case. *That* I could deal with. The glass case was secured with a small combination lock. Turning the numbers to the right combination, it clicked open and I folded back the lid. With my back firmly turned, I busied myself by emptying Bree's pirate display. I needed to install new things designed to evoke the history of the town. I returned the pirate books to their shelves and tipped the paste crystals into a plastic tub, which I stowed in my desk for another day. Searching the office, I was hoping to find some ephemera linked to the town history that I'd previously tucked away. I spotted a collection of photographs and a few other items. Both pleased and distracted at my discovery, I took them upstairs, arranging them delicately in the display case.

"Books," I murmured, laughing to myself when I realized what was missing. I turned around, looking for the local history section, and glimpsed the dark stain before quickly looking away again. I skirted around it as I went to collect the books and averted my eyes so as not to see it on my return journey.

When I finished, I closed the case and secured the lock. Turning around, I fixed my stare on the floor. Someone was calling my name but I couldn't answer; I could only gaze vacantly at the stain.

"Sara? Sara, are you okay?"

I turned around, seeing Jason walking towards me. He held a coffee cup in each hand and a paper bag from the café. Concern clouded his normally handsome face. "I called you... Sara?"

I couldn't hold it in. A tear rolled down my cheek and my face instantly crumpled.

Jason set the cups on the low console and rushed towards me. His arms wrapped around me in a tight hug, using one hand to tenderly stroke my hair. I buried my face into his chest, holding on to him as my unshed tears finally rushed out.

CHAPTER SIXTEEN

"I'm sorry. I don't know what happened."

Jason and I sat on the top step of the staircase, both of us watching the blue, yellow, and red light as it spread across the toes of our shoes. Our hands were wrapped around the coffee cups he returned with. My shivering had almost subsided and I felt drained.

"You were upset. It's natural," he said, bumping his knee against mine, and offering me a reassuring smile.

"I felt so cold," I said, my chin still trembling.

"I think that was mostly fear. It's not that cold in here."

"You are pretty hot," I said, turning to him. My eyes widened when his eyebrows rose and I realized how I sounded. "No, I meant, you are so warm. What are you? A werewolf?" I asked, thinking about how nice his radiant heat felt pressed against me as I sobbed onto his chest.

"Maybe," Jason laughed, stroking his chin. "You should see me on a weekend before I shave. Putting that aside, are you sure you want to be here? You don't have to torture yourself."

"I'm not. It just hit me all at once when I saw..." I trailed off and began nodding toward the area by the bookshelves where I'd found Bree only days before. Except for the stain, it seemed like nothing at all happened, much less a murder. "I'm okay now. Thank you. And thank you for the coffee."

"There're some muffins too. I didn't know if you had eaten breakfast yet."

"I have, but if Candice made them, I simply can't refuse!"

"The lady at Coffee Corner? With the dark hair?"

"That's her."

"Then yes, they are. I hate to confess my secret addiction to her baked goodies. I might leave Calendar ten pounds heavier than when I arrived." Jason laughed. He reached for the paper bag and passed it to me. I opened it, inhaling the sugary scent, but I didn't reach inside. Treats like these deserved a better setting. Instead, I rolled the top of the bag closed and set it by Jason's feet. "You don't want one?" he cajoled.

"Maybe in a few minutes."

"I can stay and help," offered Jason. He set down his cup and took my hand. "You don't have to do whatever you're attempting to do by yourself. What are you doing anyway?"

I thought about telling Jason I was throwing a party to which he wasn't invited, since he was indirectly the reason we were throwing it in the first place, but I decided against it. Somehow, it seemed too mean. Plus, it wasn't Jason's fault that the firm he worked for made a deal with the council to buy the land where the library was situated. He was just the unenviable one assigned to carry out their orders. Except, the little voice in my head pointed out, he could have said no. I sighed. No, he probably couldn't. He was only doing his job and had no idea how much the library meant to the town. Or what it meant to me.

"Yoo-hoo!" cooed a familiar voice I knew only too well.

I pulled my hand from Jason's abruptly, standing up so fast, I nearly tumbled down the stairs. Instantly, Jason's hands were on me again, holding me steady. I looked up at him, my heart beating faster when he gazed at me. I dared to cast an eye toward his lips, wondering what it would be like to kiss him.

"There you are!"

Lifting my eyes from Jason, the moment was shattered and I took a step away. My cheeks were already a deep shade of pink as I looked down. "Hi, Mom," I called out to her when my mother approached the base of the staircase.

"I have the coffee and tea urns in the car if you... oh, hello," she said, catching sight of Jason.

I wasn't expecting to make any introductions today, but my mother waited patiently, apparently expecting one. "Mom, this is Jason Rees. Jason, this is my mother. Nadine Cutler."

Jason hurried down the stairs, extending his hand politely. "Hello, Mrs. Cutler," he said, as she reciprocated with her hand, pumping his enthusiastically.

"I didn't realize the library was already open again," said Mom.

"It isn't," I said, taking a moment to collect our cups and the muffin bag from where we left them on the steps. "Jason just stopped by with coffee."

"You must be the nice, young man who took my daughter to dinner." Mom hung onto his hand, fixing him with a "you can tell me everything" look.

"Actually no. I haven't had the pleasure yet," said Jason. Behind him, I shook my head frantically, wishing my mother were silent.

"Ah," said Mom, blundering on. "Are you here to help with the party preparations for tonight?"

"I don't believe so, I haven't been invited," said Jason without looking at me.

I squirmed, and the ensuing awkwardness made me wish I could climb into a book and disappear. "It's not a party, Mom, and Jason isn't here to help. He wants to close the library."

"*You're* the man who wants to relocate the library to a new building that doesn't leak and creak?" said Mom. "You're not nearly as awful as my daughter made out. Will the new library have modern heating?"

"Mom, you can give Jason his hand back now," I reminded her, waiting until she dropped his hand.

"I'm sure the library will be everything the town expects it to be," he said. "I'll see myself out. Nice to meet you, Mrs. Cutler. Bye, Sara."

"Bye," I muttered weakly as he took off without waiting for me to hand him his barely-drunk coffee.

"He seems nice," said Mom. "Why didn't you invite him tonight?"

"Because *I'm* trying to save the library and *he* wants to close it! He *will* close it too if we don't get all the support we need."

My mother looked around and frowned. "Is that really such a bad thing?"

"Yes! Mom! Look at this place. It's so beautiful. It just needs fixing and preserving, not being torn down."

My mother cast a critical eye over the library. "It could use some new books too."

"We have a budget for new books," I pointed out, and not for the first time. "If you ever borrowed a book, you'd know that already."

"You know I don't have any spare time for reading. How you ended up becoming such a bookworm, I'll never know."

"It'll remain a mystery to us both," I agreed. "Take me to the urns. I'll get them set up and return them tomorrow."

"You know, maybe we shouldn't call them urns, given the circumstances."

"What do you mean?"

"I mean, some people associate urns with the vessels to hold the cremated remains of dead bodies." Mom pointed to the ceiling. "If you keep talking about them as *urns*, people might mistake what you mean."

"The police already took Bree's body away. They certainly don't plan to bring her back!"

"Has anyone appeared to claim her yet?"

"None that I know about."

"How sad that there's no one to care."

"We don't know that for sure. Detective Logan is still looking for her family."

"Is Detective Logan coming to the party tonight? He's rather handsome and still single, from what I hear."

I sighed. "What's your point, Mom?"

"You could do a lot worse than dating a handsome detective."

I rolled my eyes. "I am not even remotely interested in Detective Logan! He's very nice but no more my type than I am his."

"Oh? And what about Tom?"

"Tom is very nice," I told her, ushering her towards the door. "We've only been on one date though and it was... pleasant."

"Pleasant? Is that all you can say? Can't you think of anything else to say about him?"

"He is very nice," I repeated.

"And Jason?"

"Jason? He's..." I stopped and began thinking about him as a man. Jason was more than handsome. He was also warm, generous, and kind-hearted. His unexpected presence a few nights ago might have even saved me from Bree's killer. He also picked me up when he could have left me stranded at the roadside. Well, not exactly stranded but definitely in need of assistance. We ate brunch together and talked almost non-stop. When I was pressed up against his chest just a few minutes ago, he smelled amazing. His mint-fresh scent still clung to me. He held my hand and made my heart race.

"He's planning to close this place down," I said with finality and a wave of disappointment I wished I didn't feel. There was no point in me thinking about Jason at all. Not when as soon as he finished his job here, he would pack up and leave. I would probably never see

Jason again. A few days ago, that thought would have made me happy. Now, however, it made me feel strangely heavy.

"And give you a whole new library," Mom pointed out again. "Not many men would do that."

"It's his firm, not him."

"So why are you blaming him?"

"Why are we even talking about this?" I asked. I shivered as we stepped outside into the cold.

"Because I want to see you happy."

"I am happy, except that my friend was killed, my job is being threatened and my favorite building is going to be torn down."

"Is it too much to ask if there's a second date with the other man on the horizon?"

"There might be a lunch date. We haven't confirmed it yet." When we did, I would definitely ask him what kind of business had brought him to town and how long he planned on staying.

"Did you invite him to the party?"

"Again, it's not a party. It's an event; but yes, he said he would come."

"Hmm," said Mom but this time, she beeped open the car and reached into the backseat to pass me one of the heavy urns. I wrapped my hands under it and hefted it inside. Placing it on the big, wooden console that I usually reserved for an assortment of pamphlets and bookmarks, I returned to the car for the second urn and set it next to the first.

"Thanks again for bringing these."

"Sara? Are you in there?" Candice stepped inside, craning her head around the door, and smiling when she spotted me. She held up two large grocery bags, that made a clinking sound inside them. "Ally at the Belle Rose restaurant asked me to bring these, and she also said she'll try and stop by later."

"What are they?"

"Wine! A dozen bottles! She is also letting you borrow the glasses they use for parties at no charge."

"That is very generous of her!" I exclaimed, hurrying over to relieve her of one of the heavy bags. I had only spoken to Ally McKellar a few times and she never visited the library. All I knew about her was that she returned home to Calendar to open Belle Rose after moving away years before. Her generosity was completely unexpected and utterly pleasing. "I never expected anything like this."

"When I told her about the event tonight, she said she wanted to help. Isn't it great? I'll make the snacks this afternoon and bring them over later. Shall I bring the wine glasses inside?"

"Yes, please," I agreed, nodding enthusiastically. I could hardly believe my luck. The tea and coffee would have made pleasing refreshments, but the wine and snacks almost guaranteed the guests would be very happy.

"Lots of people said they'll come," Candice continued. "Jaclyn insisted on taking over at the café and I know she's telling everyone that comes in to show their support. I might have to bake some more items, otherwise we'll probably run out."

"How many is a lot?" I asked.

"Oh, everyone I spoke with!" Candice grinned. "Isn't it wonderful how everyone pitches in to support the library? Those pamphlets you and that handsome guy distributed around town really got people talking about it. I think you'll have a great turnout tonight. Do you want me to put the red wine on the table? We could put the white wine on the porch to chill?"

"Sounds great and yes, we're setting everything up on this table."

Candice added her grocery bag to the table and unpacked the wine before hurrying outside to collect her other items. My mother raised her eyebrow at the accumulating bottles. "Sure looks like you're having a party," she said. She leaned in and kissed my cheek, and we hugged briefly. "See you tonight."

"Isn't your mom staying to help?" asked Candice, returning with several cardboard boxes stacked in her arms. She passed them to me to unload.

"She probably has someone else to organize," I laughed. "But she'll be here tonight."

"Was that Jason Rees I saw outside in his car?"

"He was here earlier," I told her, "but I thought he left already."

"Did you invite him to the party too?"

"Now you sound like my mother! No, I didn't, but my mom practically did and it got a little awkward."

"I'll bet! I know he's the big, bad villain around here right now, but I kind of like him. Although I feel guilty for admitting it."

"I know what you mean," I told her. The phone in my office began to ring and I excused myself, leaving Candice to continue bringing in the baked goods by herself.

"Calendar Library," I said on answering, expecting a patron on the other end of the line, or maybe someone inquiring about the event.

"Is this Sara?" asked the woman. Her voice had a slightly Southern accent.

"Yes, this is she. How may I help you?"

"I think you know my sister," she said, almost hesitantly. "Her name is Brittany but I think you might know her as Bree. I hope you don't mind me calling. I spoke with Detective Logan and he told me my sister was working for you when she..." The woman broke off, sobbing.

"I am so sorry," I told her, my heart twinging with an unexpected pang. News of Bree's family was something I hardly dared to hope for after the visit with her former roommate. "Yes, Bree and I worked together. I'm so sorry about what happened."

"I can hardly believe it. It's just awful. I can't imagine anyone who would hurt Brittany. I thought she had gotten her life together... and for this to happen... It's so sad."

"I can't imagine how hard this must be for you and your family."

"Oh, it's just us," said the woman. "Brittany and I haven't seen our parents in a long time and she and I weren't very close. She probably never even mentioned me. I'm afraid I was pretty hard on her for not improving her life more so we didn't keep in touch often. That affected our relationship."

"I'm sure she understood," I murmured, unsure that Bree did. I searched my mind for any mention of a sister, but if Bree ever spoke of her, I couldn't remember when. Besides, everything she did tell me was a lie.

"That is so kind of you. I wondered if we could meet? I'm coming into town tomorrow and I would appreciate it so much. I'd really like your help in trying to make some sense of all this."

"Absolutely," I agreed, knowing I couldn't possibly refuse. "When would be a good time?"

"Can I call you as soon as I get there? I couldn't find a local bed and breakfast with a vacancy so I'm planning on staying at a motel just a short distance from town. We could meet there or somewhere else if you like?"

"Wherever is convenient for you. Let's exchange phone numbers and then you can call me anytime," I offered. "I didn't get your name?"

"Angela Daniels. We don't have the same surname because I'm married," she explained. "Thank you so much for your help."

"If there is anything I can do at all, please call me," I urged her. "I can't imagine how devastating this must be for you. I considered Bree my friend."

"I am very happy to hear she made a friend. I can't wait to meet you and learn all about Bree's life there," she told me. "See you tomorrow."

I replaced the handset and leaned back in my chair. Finally, someone who knew Bree! Angela might have been looking forward to hearing anything I could tell her but I feared she would be disappointed when she learned how little I could say. My only hope was that Angela would be more forthcoming about the darker things Bree was mixed up in. Perhaps she even knew the boyfriend

Bree was apparently so afraid of that she ran away. Tomorrow, I hoped to find out as much as I could.

CHAPTER SEVENTEEN

"Is that where it happened?"

"Do you think the killer was still inside?"

"I wonder where the treasure is?"

I overheard the incessant questions, repressing the desire to put the owners of the whispers to rights. The steady flood of guests had initially been very pleasing. Seeing so many people show up, on such short notice too, just to support the library was wonderful, but until I actually paid attention to their comments, I naively assumed their interest was purely in saving the library. That, or to enjoy Candice's baked goods and the free wine that Ally from the Belle Rose restaurant had so generously donated.

"Why are you hiding back here?" asked Meredith. She was dressed in a very stylish pair of black trousers and a black cashmere sweater. Somehow, it made her the most glamorous person in the room. "Shouldn't you be out there rallying the troops?"

I glanced up from the glasses I was organizing, somewhat pointlessly since there was nothing wrong with their original formation. "Have you heard them?" I asked, certain that my discomfort showed.

Meredith hesitated. "Okay, yes, I've heard their chatter, but does it really matter? There will always be gossip and those that flock to it."

"But they only came tonight to gawk at the spot where a murder happened! They don't intend to even support the library in Bree's memory. It's terrible!"

"They would probably be a lot kinder about the gossip if Bree hadn't turned out to be a master criminal with millions in loot! She may have come here rather anonymously and lived quietly but everyone in town knows who she really was now."

"Did you know someone was digging in the library garden earlier? Like Bree would've stashed her loot there."

Meredith shrugged. "Who knows where she hid it? It's not like any of us guessed what she was up to when she came here. I'm sure it'll be the most fascinating thing to happen in Calendar in years, maybe even decades."

I paused, reflecting on that. "I know but it doesn't make it any less... dispiriting," I settled on a word that summed up my disappointment. "I just wish most of the people came here tonight to save the library, not to speculate over the murder."

"I suggest you use the advantage, since they're here for your benefit," said Meredith. "You need to make a speech and be sure to encourage every single person to sign the petition. I can help circulate the petition for you or I can even stand at the door and pounce on people as they come in or exit."

I hesitated. Meredith had a good point. "Do you think so?"

"Absolutely! If you really want to get them to sign, stand on the staircase and refuse to let anyone pass until they add their signature."

"Why the staircase?"

"Because all these people want to have a fleeting glimpse upstairs, if you get what I mean."

I grimaced as I realized her meaning. Having done my best to hide the remaining bloodstain by sliding one of the racks to one side slightly, I shifted a small loveseat from the other end to act as an end cap for the bookcase. Between the two, I was sure nothing was still visible. Hopefully, everyone who ventured upstairs would be so distracted by the new display I fashioned by the window, they would forget about it.

It felt strange to change the last display Bree had created but it had to be done some time. Putting it off until the day the library doors had to be closed would have been much worse. While waiting for Jason to bring the coffee, I'd taken the opportunity to create an ode to the town under the glass display case. Surrounding a large sepia photograph on the day the library first opened, I added local history books and a memoir a local resident had written. I left it open to the page where he described visiting the library as a child. Some old-fashioned tickets and other little mementos that were unearthed when the floors were fixed a few years ago completed the exhibit. I thought it was charming enough to tug a few heartstrings.

"That's a really good idea," I agreed, immediately doubting myself. "But isn't that shameful trickery? If they're not sincerely concerned about the library, why would they sign it?"

"People will sign anything, given the right motivation. Plus, can you imagine the outcry when the library gets torn down and they realize they did nothing to save it when they could have?"

"Maybe they want a new fancy library with pulp fiction and audiobooks and a permanent coffee cart."

"You can put all those things here! This place will always be the most beautiful library anyone has ever seen." Meredith laid a hand on my arm. "Don't let the gossip affect you. This is your event, these people are here, and you can make them help save it." She handed me the clipboard with the scarce, few signatures on the petition, and grabbed another one for herself before turning me around and giving me a little push towards the stairs. "Go now and make that speech," she directed. "And remind them all why they're really here tonight."

Public speaking wasn't my forte, which was probably why I made a career in telling people to "shh" a lot. At least, that's what I liked to joke, but Meredith was right. The evening might not have started out as I planned but I had to take advantage of the people milling around here and the chance to let them know how losing the library would affect them. If I could turn their attendance into real signatures, I might have one last chance to save the library.

I stepped onto the staircase, turning on the fourth step. The height gave me a good overview of the crowd. I spotted my mother near the back. She was deep in conversation with several people from her gardening club. Meredith was stationed at the door and I watched her thrust the clipboard and a pen at the next couple who walked through. Candice, Jaclyn—propped up with a cane—and Grace were standing near the desk with wine glasses in hand. My boss, Marta, from the council, nibbled a cookie and waved when she saw me looking her way. I waved back, smiling, and glad she had come. A group of teens stood away from their parents and I recalled when they helped Bree with the children's Christmas story day. It was only a few weeks before. I recognized many faces and saw many other unfamiliar ones too. Tom stood by the new books shelf and waved to me. I smiled, returning his wave, and happy he had come. I was even more pleased that my mother hadn't accosted him.

"Hello," I called out, waving my hands to grab everyone's attention. "Hello! Thank you so much for coming here tonight on such short notice," I continued loudly. The noise lessened before puttering away as the expectant faces turned to me. "I am so thrilled to see so many familiar faces this evening here to support the historic Calendar Library. Next year will mark our hundredth-year anniversary—" I paused for the smattering of applause "—but we won't make it unless we have your continued support. Many of you already know that the library needs some repairs; and lack of funding is, unfortunately, making that difficult. The council received an offer proposing that the land on which this library stands to be sold for the imminent destruction of our precious library to make way for more housing." I paused for some grumbles and tried to ignore the loudly whispered comments about having more new diggers excavating the land and who might find the buried treasure if that happened.

"I know, it's very disappointing. In all fairness, I must also tell you that the developer has offered us a new library on another site in town. This is in return for tearing down this beautiful, old building that so many of us have used and admired throughout our lives. We're here tonight to protest its demolition, and pledge our fight for our library. We must join voices to say that we don't want a new library! We don't want to have new homes built on this dedicated community site! Calendar says no to any new development!" I let my voice rise as I pumped my fist in the air. Applause followed my speech along with a few cries of support.

I continued, the audience momentum spurring me on. "Thank you so much for turning out in this rainy weather to show your support. We don't have much time to save the library, so please sign the petitions that are being circulated and make your voices heard. Together, we can do this. Thank you." I smiled as another round of applause echoed through the old building before I moved down a couple of steps so I still blocked the staircase.

"Good speech," said Antonio, craning his head to look around me.

"Thanks so much for distributing the flyers advertising the party. You're welcome to go up," I told him as I thrust the petition forwards. He grabbed the pen and signed before I edged out of his way, repeating the same thing to more than a dozen people who eagerly tried to get past me. From the door, Meredith gave me the thumbs up.

I shook hands and commiserated with the patrons, agreeing with them that we could probably afford to get a coffee cart too, and one of those new e-book lending machines to launch the library into the current century. I talked about volunteer positions to the teens and discussed popular fiction versus classical literature with the Calendar Ladies Book Club. Not once, however, did I let a person go upstairs without adding their signature to my petition.

"This is a good turnout," said Marta. Big beads hung around her neck in her usual flamboyant style. "I didn't realize everyone loved the library so much."

"Everyone has fond memories of this place," said an elderly gentleman as he edged past us. I held out my petition and he signed it quickly. "So much has happened here," he murmured, his gaze turning upstairs. I stepped aside and let him pass, in case he decided to expand on that.

"We even had our first kiss out there in the garden," said the woman following him.

"That is so lovely." I beamed as I held out the petition.

"If you can get enough signatures to show this place has community interest and value, the council might listen. Good work, Sara," said Marta. "I'll speak with you soon."

"Thanks for coming!"

"So this is the famous library," said Tom, leaning in to kiss my cheek before looking up and around. "I've gotta say, it's some kinda place."

"Do you like it?" I asked, following his lingering gaze to the ornate cornicing and the grandfather clock.

"Who wouldn't?" he asked. "It's charming."

"I'm glad you think so. Can I get you to sign the petition?" I offered him the pen and he took it, signing with a flourish.

"Thank you, Tom... Nicholson," I said, turning the clipboard to read his signature. "We appreciate your support."

"I thought I could take you for a drink later to congratulate you on your success," he said. "I know I had to renege on the offer of lunch but I intend to make up for it. What do you say?"

I frowned, knowing I would have to disappoint him. Not because I resented him calling to say he couldn't make lunch after all. The free time became very useful. I wasn't so stressed out to prepare for the library event and distribute some more flyers. I brushed away the knowledge that I'd spent more of that time thinking about Jason than I had about Tom. Instead, I plastered a smile on my face. "I would love to but I need to clean up before we reopen tomorrow and I don't know how long that will take."

"Can I help? I know my way around a mop and a trashcan." He smiled broadly, and was effortlessly charming.

"That is so kind of you to offer but I already have a couple friends who said they would help out and I wouldn't want to waste your time. Maybe we could have lunch or meet after work tomorrow?" I added, remembering that Bree's sister planned on calling me as soon as she got to town.

"Sounds perfect. Hey, did you hear anymore of that talk about someone hiding treasure here?"

I groaned. "Not you too! It's all I hear."

"I plead innocence." He held his hands up and laughed. "I couldn't help overhearing a few conversations. Is this about the girl you knew?"

"Yes. Some people believe she hid stolen treasure here since she worked here for a few months."

"Do you think she did?"

"Look around—" I waved my hands at the interior, "—do you see any jewels?"

"No, but I'm guessing they wouldn't be anywhere obvious. Do you have any secret drawers or hidden rooms? Maybe look in the air vents or loose floorboards?" He winked.

"I'm pretty sure if you ask around, someone will admit that they already tried that. I caught Mr. Riley examining the air vents and my mother saw Mrs. Mendez taking a good look at my desk."

"Amateurs," laughed Tom. "I have to say how fascinating it is to see all of these regular, supposedly normal people suddenly turning into treasure hunters."

"Hopefully, Detective Logan will ensure they calm down soon." I looked around, wondering if the detective had made an appearance. I was disappointed to see he hadn't although it was probably a good thing. The crowd would have pestered him.

"He have any leads yet?"

I shook my head. "I don't think so but he's probably getting annoyed when people keep calling the police station to complain about random holes being dug anywhere Bree went or might have gone."

"Poor guy." Tom looked around. "I can see you should mingle and unless you need a ride home, I'm going to take off soon. I need to finish up some work emails. Unless I hear anymore salubrious gossip about the treasure, in which case, I might stick around. Did I tell you how fascinating it is?"

I couldn't help laughing at his undisguised interest. "I'm glad we can provide you with some entertainment while you're in town!"

"More than that," he said, taking my hand and pressing his lips to my knuckles as I blushed. "If I'd known how charming this town was, I would have made my way here years ago. Good night, Sara." At the door, he turned and waved.

"Please tell me that's my future son-in-law," said my mother. I jumped when I found her on the other side of the staircase, looking thrilled. "Is that Tom?"

"Yes. He came to support the library."

"Isn't that mighty town-minded of him?! It's a good turnout. You must be very pleased."

"Very. I filled one page of signatures already since my speech."

"There's a lot of gossip about Bree. She turned out to be a strange one," Mom continued. "Who ever would have thought a career criminal would choose our town to hide out from the law? Everyone's speculating about where she could've hidden the loot."

"You too?"

"Me? No. I have better things to do than tunnel around town with a spade. You don't need to worry about the garden here anymore. I heard that Bree was once spotted over by that new housing development outside of town."

"Really? When?"

"Oh, I think it was last week sometime. Apparently, she was seen out there late at night. Probably digging up her loot before she made a run for it."

"Why would anyone bury treasure at a construction site? That doesn't make any sense."

"It wouldn't but Bree was seen leaving the show home. That's been finished now for a couple months; I don't imagine she was looking to buy a house here, do you?"

"Not that I know of."

"My point exactly. Is that Candice with more of those delicious little brownies?" asked Mom, shooting off before I could ask her what else she'd heard about Bree, or even if she signed the petition.

The event continued for another hour until someone made some noise about a severe weather warning. With the wine all gone, and only crumbs left on the cake plates, the crowd dispersed quickly until there were only three of us left. Most of the debris was confined to the first floor, so Candice, Meredith and I grabbed trash bags and quickly scooped up the litter. I returned the used glasses to their cardboard carry boxes and bundled up the wine bottles. Candice emptied the tea and coffee urns and stowed the hospitality tray of sugar and creamers away.

"You really don't have to stay," I told them, nodding to the rain lashing against the windows.

"I would not leave you to clear up alone," said Meredith.

"And I'm your ride home," said Candice. "Plus, guess what I hid to one side!" she added, reaching for a half bottle of wine that she snuck behind the desk. "Let's clean up and toast to a very successful evening. Everyone loved the displays and I overheard Marta talking about doing another town fundraiser to pay for all the repairs the library needs."

"And we gained over three hundred signatures tonight," said Meredith. "We already have more than a thousand in just the past two weeks. I think we can get that number higher if we keep asking people."

"But is it enough?" I wondered.

"Even if it isn't, you tried your best," said Meredith. She poured the wine into three clean glasses and passed a glass to each of us. "To Sara, for throwing this party and reminding us all why we love the library so much."

"Cheers," I said, taking a sip.

Behind me the door creaked open, the noise followed by a footstep. I turned, thoroughly surprised to see Jason.

"Hi," he said.

"Hi. What are you doing here?"

"The party's over," pointed out Candice.

"I know," he said before turning his attention to me. "I thought I wouldn't be welcome."

"Why not? You only want to knock the library down," said Candice sarcastically.

"He's only doing his job," I said.

"Then he should really hold a debate and invite everyone. Then we can all tell him what we think of his stinking plan."

"Okay," said Jason, nodding. "Let's look into doing that. Until then, I came to see if you needed a ride home. I figured your car might still be in the shop."

"It is."

"I'm her ride," said Candice.

"I think we need to clean upstairs," said Meredith.

"But we already..." Candice broke off as Meredith steered her upstairs, leaving Jason and me alone. It wasn't subtle but ever-so-helpful.

"I appreciate the offer," I told him, "but she really is my ride home."

"You're okay locking up?" He glanced up to where I was sure Candice and Meredith hovered just out of sight.

"I'm sure we'll be fine together, and the rain is so bad right now, I doubt anyone will be on the street at all."

"Okay, then." Jason hesitated. "Would you like to have lunch with me tomorrow?"

"So you can pick my brains on how the petition is coming along?" I asked, but immediately regretted blurting out the question when I saw Jason's face fall.

"Actually, I thought we could talk about the library's current needs."

"I didn't mean to be rude. I already made plans but perhaps you'd prefer to talk to my boss, Marta?"

"Nothing you can get out of?" He waited, the silence between us only punctuated by the ticking of the grandfather clock. I was sure at any moment, it would chime midnight and I had the awful feeling I would turn into a pumpkin. "Another date?" he surmised. "Must be some lucky guy."

"Jason, I..." I started, ready to tell him it wasn't a date, but instead I was waiting for Angela Daniels to call. I stopped when he stepped nearer, closing the gap between us. I could feel the heat from him, and the minty scent I inhaled earlier swarmed my senses. Then his mouth was on mine, my lips tingling as the kiss deepened. He pulled me closer and my arms circled his neck. I held onto him, my heart racing. Shivers shot down my spine at the intensity of the kiss. Breathlessly, he stepped back, breaking us apart.

"I've wanted to do that since the first moment I laid eyes on you," he said. Before I could respond, he turned and left, closing the door behind him.

From upstairs, I heard an "Oooh!" and Candice giggled.

I touched my fingers to my still tingling lips and knew exactly what she meant.

CHAPTER EIGHTEEN

The next day, Bree's sister called me. It was a few minutes after eleven and I had already been at the library for two hours, serving a steady stream of customers. It was an unusually busy morning and, like last night's party, I was certain it had nothing to do with anyone desperately needing a new book. No, they were the gawkers who couldn't make it to the party. Although I accepted the condolences with grace, and promised I would pass them along to the family, I was getting more than a little tired of the questions. When Angela called, I was good and ready for a break.

"I already checked into the motel I told you about. It's ten miles outside of Calendar," she told me. "It's not that great but I didn't want to cancel it only to discover there was nowhere else to book; and it would be too strange to stay at Brittany's apartment."

"I understand. Are you planning a long visit?"

"No, I don't think so. Just long enough to speak to the police detective in charge of the case and, of course, arrange for Brittany's burial." She sniffled and fell into silence, broken every few seconds with strange, little hiccups that I assumed were probably sobs.

"I'm so sorry you have to do that." I wished there were more I could do to help her and I resolved to offer my assistance when we met in person.

"Someone has to," Angela sighed. "I don't know anyone else to talk to. I think you're the only person who knew Bree in town."

"She talked to a lot of people but we were also colleagues and I thought we were friends."

"What do you mean?"

I hesitated, not wanting to cause offense. I settled on what I hoped weren't hurtful words. "I don't think she told me the truth about a lot of things."

"That sounds like my sister," Angela said in a resigned tone. "She told a lot of lies. I was very worried about her. I'm afraid she must have gotten into something way over her head."

I thought about the missing jewels and decided she was probably right; but I didn't have to say anything because she continued, "I think she screwed someone over... I really hoped she'd straighten out her life, you know? She seemed so happy in her job."

"You spoke to her recently?"

"Yes, we usually kept in touch." Angela paused. "She didn't mention me at all, did she?"

"No." I winced as I said it, knowing she probably would want to hear something nicer.

She sighed again. "Well, anyway, I'm here now. I'm looking forward to meeting you."

"I'm taking my lunch break soon. Why don't I drive over to you?" I smiled, glad my car had been returned this morning before I left for work. Besides, I didn't want to put her to any effort. I wondered where she'd driven from and how long it took her, knowing that when she got here, there would be no happy reunion.

"That sounds great but I don't want to put you to any trouble. Let's not meet at the motel because it's not that nice. Do you know somewhere else convenient?"

I reached for a pen. "I know somewhere near you," I told her. "Do you have a pen?"

~

Angela Daniels didn't share a lot of physical features with her sister. We were sitting across from each other in the Mountain View Restaurant and gardens. Like the name suggested, it boasted a glorious view of the currently snow-capped mountains. In the summer, the restaurant spilled out onto a paved terrace that came alive with glorious planting. It was a nice place and rather quiet, since most people looking for a quick lunch would have aimed for one of the cafés or restaurants dotted around the main square. I didn't want to subject Angela to any undue gossip while she was visiting, nor did I want to answer any more of the locals' questions about her sister.

I knew Angela realized I noticed the difference in her appearance, compared to Bree, when she explained, "You might have guessed we're half-sisters. Bree took after her mom and I took after our dad. She got the curves, I got the height. She also got her Mom's brown eyes and I got Dad's green ones. I went to live with Dad in the south so even our accents are different. To be brutally honest, we didn't share a lot in common at all."

"Is that why you lost touch?" I asked. I warmed my hands on the coffee cup as I looked across the table at Angela.

Angela took a sip then set her cup down. "Not really. Mostly because Brittany was always making bad choices and I couldn't bail her out anymore. I heard she was hiding out here," she said, looking around as if Bree might jump out from the trees anytime.

"You must have spoken to Detective Logan," I surmised. "He told me she was wanted by the police."

Angela sighed heavily, apparently her go-to reaction when talking about her sister. "He told me she stole something and hid it. Jewels. It's just so appalling. He said Brittany was involved in stealing them, and must have been in some kind of gang. I should have tried harder," she sniffled again, her face crumpling as she reached into her purse and pulled out a small pack of tissues.

I reached across the table and gave her hand a squeeze. "You mustn't blame yourself. Bree was old enough to make her own decisions, including bad ones."

"I know that's true. It's just hard to reconcile the sweet, little girl I grew up with to the woman she became."

"It must be very hard," I mumbled, unsure of what else to say.

"I hate to think that she brought so much trouble to this beautiful town."

"Most of the residents are a little shocked. It's not exactly the kind of place where—" I stopped before the word *criminal* spilt from my lips.

"It's okay. We don't have to pretend. Brittany *was* a criminal. I understand you were her closest friend?" she said.

I nodded. "I thought we were but now I have to question everything I thought I knew."

"That's natural. Sara, I just can't help thinking she might have used you while she was here. I know, I know —" Holding her hands up as if she were pleading with me to hear her out, she continued, "—It's not a pleasant thought but I can't help thinking she could have used you to hide the jewels, in which case, you could be in serious danger. Forgive me for saying so."

"You're not the first to think that. Someone already dug up the library gardens."

Angela's hand flew to her mouth. "That's awful! Do you think they found anything?"

"No, I think they were scared off. I doubt Bree would have hidden them there anyway. The ground would have been too hard since she arrived in Calendar. Not exactly favorable for digging and hiding treasure," I explained.

"No, I guess not. Maybe she hid them somewhere in her apartment."

"Could be, but I think Detective Logan turned the apartment inside-out more than once."

"He does sound like a very thorough man."

"He's very good but we don't get a lot of crime here. I'm sure Detective Logan is as shocked as the rest of us."

"I'm sure. He must have searched the library too and anywhere else Brittany liked to frequent."

"He probably searched the library when I found Bree," I decided, "but he wouldn't have known he was looking for a something then, just *someone*."

"That's interesting. I heard a rumor that the library was to be sold. Is that true?"

"Unfortunately, it might be. I've been campaigning to save it, along with other residents here, but I dare not predict the outcome. If we don't succeed, the library will be torn down and replaced with houses."

Angela shook her head sadly. "And all traces of Brittany will be gone. Where else did Brittany like to go around town? I'd like to see her frequent haunts, like I'm retracing her footsteps. Is that strange?"

"No, I think it's nice but I'm not sure how helpful I can be. She spent a lot of her time at the library and since it was winter, the rest of her time at her apartment. We had lunch at the Coffee Corner Café a few times, and I know she liked the candy store. I guess she visited some of the other shops. I'll write their names for you." Jotting down the names on the notepad I carried in my purse, I passed them to Angela. As I did, I thought of something else. "Someone mentioned seeing her out by the Bayview Drive housing development, which is just outside town. You must have driven past it on your way here. I can't imagine what she was doing there though."

Angela frowned. "Me neither. She never mentioned any desire to buy a house and never showed any interest in construction."

"It's probably nothing. Maybe she took a wrong turn."

"Probably," agreed Angela.

I checked my watch, seeing my lunch break was almost over although I still hadn't eaten. Fortunately, I brought a packed lunch to the library. I really didn't want to sit at my desk eating it while more patrons wandered in. It didn't seem professional. "I have to go, "I told her, trying to sound as apologetic as I felt, "but I hope I was helpful."

"You were," she assured me. She got up and hugged me quickly. "Thank you so much for taking the time to meet me."

"Call me if you need anything else. Anything at all. I'd like to send flowers to Bree's funeral, if that's okay with you? Regardless of what she did, I will always consider her a friend and I'm sad she's gone."

I left Angela at Mountain View and drove back to the library. After a ten-minute lunch, most of which was spent musing on how disappointed Bree's sister looked during our conversation. I unlocked the library doors again.

A steady stream of traffic continued throughout the afternoon and I added a lot more signatures to my petition. I answered even more questions about Bree and tried not to bristle at the collective morbid curiosity of some people. They felt compelled to leave their homes just to view a "real, live crime scene" as more than one eager spectator put it. By the time I'd ushered out the last of the lingering gawkers, I was glad to close the door. Instead of relaxing like I sometimes did or perusing the books or setting up for the next event, I grabbed my coat and purse. With my keys ready in my hand, I quickly locked up, hurrying to my car.

Instead of turning for home, I realized I was pointing the car towards the housing development. The idea of Bree going there kept niggling me all day. The more I thought about it, the more I decided I was wrong about Bree taking a wrong turn or ending up there by accident. My mom said Bree was looking around. Since Meredith overheard a conversation that she wasn't planning on staying in town, Bree had to be there for another reason.

The only reason I could think of for Bree to be prowling at a half-built housing development was to hide something.

The rain had let up by the time I turned onto Bayview Drive, following the curve of the road until I reached the show home. It was currently the only completed house in the development. Lights shone throughout the house and a smart Lexus was parked in the driveway. Probably the realtor's, I decided, or a very nice suggestion from the developers.

I parked at the curb under the streetlamp, after noticing the dark night rolling in, and grabbed my purse, hurrying into the house. I knocked and a middle-aged woman in a gray pantsuit came to the door. "I normally leave the door open in a show home," she explained as she ushered me inside, "but it's just too cold. I'm Gwendolyn Cooper, the realtor. Are you looking to buy?"

I hesitated, then decided to play along. "Maybe. A friend of mine came by recently and told me how nice this house was. She made me promise to come by and take a look; and I can see already that she was right!"

"Wait until you see the rest of the house! There's an eat-in kitchen with a pantry and mud room leading to the yard. A living room and formal dining room plus, a small study." She reeled off a sales patter that she'd clearly relayed a hundred times before. I nodded, following her as she took off for the living room. The house was lovely. Someone had cleverly staged it as a family home, the type I normally only glimpsed in magazines. It was nicely appointed with all manner of smart technology and appliances.

"Do you have a family? Children?" Gwendolyn asked, glancing over her shoulder as we left the kitchen. We were heading for the stairs in the entry.

"No," I said.

"Oh, you're just starting a family?" she decided. "Then you will love the nursery upstairs. This is a house where you can start a family and not worry about the future need to move. Many of our families call our homes their forever homes. Your friend probably told you all about it already."

"Yes, she did," I said, seizing on that. "Perhaps you remember her? Brown hair to about here, curvy, and a little shorter than me?"

"Oh, yes, I think I do remember her. She was looking for a place to live after she got married," she said. "Lovely young lady. Britt, wasn't it?"

Britt had to be short for Brittany. Another alias. "That's her," I said.

"She was interested in several of our lots. If you buy off plan, you can pick your choice of fixtures and finishes from our catalogue and customize many other details too."

"Was that what Britt wanted?"

"We briefly discussed it but she was mostly interested in how long it would take until the development was built. I told her our first homes would be available in six months and the rest by the end of the year. It's understandable really. A lot of people don't want to live on a construction site, or feel really alone at night being surrounded by vacant lots. Wouldn't it be great if you both moved here together? You could even get adjoining lots!"

"Mmm," I murmured, knowing that would never happen. Suddenly, I wondered if Bree ever considered hiding her jewels here, since the development would have remained empty for some time. If she planned on a quick departure, she could have easily gotten access to them, or even grabbed them as she left town. "Apart from the show home, are there any other houses that are finished?"

"There's four more on this street, but they're essentially no more than shells. Being of the same layout as this one, what you see here is achievable there. Three have already sold but the fourth is still available."

"Has this house sold yet?" I asked.

"No, not yet and it isn't available for sale either. The owners of the development need to use it as a show home. However, if you're interested, I can add your name to the list? I'm sure you'll get a great deal on all the furniture too if you want it. This is the master bedroom," she said as we stepped into a beautiful room and her attention reverted to square footage, closets, and "magnificent views."

By the time we returned downstairs, another couple had entered and the saleswoman greeted them by name. I guessed it wasn't their first visit. After saying my goodbyes, I took a brochure and assured Gwendolyn that the house was better than great and I would think seriously about it. As I walked back to my car, I turned and looked around the street. She told me the other almost finished homes were on the same street. Since I had the rare opportunity to see them a little further along, I would because they all stood in a row.

As I stared at them, I wondered which one Bree would have chosen for a hiding place. Without realizing it, I started to walk towards them, stepping onto the road since the sidewalks hadn't yet been installed. In no time, I was outside the first one. The doors and windows were recently installed and I walked up to it. I tested the handle and found it locked. A path was created although there wasn't any other landscaping. I followed it around to the back and tested the kitchen door. Also locked.

The moon dipped behind a large cloud, casting the yard into darkness. I shivered, suddenly aware of how vulnerable I was and alone. I scrabbled in my purse for my key ring and pulled it out, pressing the button on the little flashlight that was attached to the fob. A small beam danced on the ground, just enough to illuminate where I walked. The last thing I needed was a sprained ankle. Back on the road, I looked again at the other three houses. A car was parked by the furthest house, and the tail end was barely peeking out. I decided it was probably one of the builders and dismissed it.

Something wasn't right in my thinking but I ignored it.

I thought about the locked doors and decided they probably weren't a problem to Bree. I had no idea what criminal activities she might've mastered but I figured picking a lock was probably a pretty basic one. Plus, if she were planning to run out of town, she probably wouldn't have cared if she had to smash her way into the house to retrieve her haul. Except, how could she be sure that the houses would still be empty? Plus, if the houses still had to be fitted out, how could she be sure that the builders wouldn't stumble across her loot?

It was obvious to me: she couldn't have been sure.

I looked over to the show home and almost laughed. Here I was looking for Bree's treasure when I'd been so cross about other people doing exactly that! Except I was curious about Bree's movements more than what she hid. As I stepped forwards, I noticed two more cars were parked behind mine. The couple I'd already seen were leaving. They were smiling and shaking hands before walking to their car. They climbed in and made a U-turn. The realtor waited for them to drive off before closing the door, turning to speak to someone inside.

That was it!

That's what I missed.

There was only one home on the entire lot that was guaranteed not to be tampered with any further, and I had just been inside it. If Bree wanted to hide her jewels, she could have easily done so inside the show home. All she had to do was hide the jewels inside an air vent, or a toilet cistern, anywhere really, since it was very doubtful that anyone would do anything further to the house or discover her haul by chance. She could walk back in there anytime she liked and retrieve them.

I stepped forwards towards the path and stopped when I heard a tiny noise. A footfall was somewhere near me.

I looked up, realizing that someone was trying the front door, just as I had minutes ago.

"What..." I started to say but the figure rushed at me, fists raised.

I screamed as the first blow knocked me to the damp floor.

CHAPTER NINETEEN

"Sara?" The voice could have been a thousand miles away.

Then it came again, this time repeating my name a little louder. "Sara?"

"Uggh-nnn."

"Sara, can you hear me?"

"She's coming around," said another voice, a female one.

"Sara? You're okay. I found you."

I recognized the voice. Clinging to the sound, I blinked slowly, forcing my eyes open. I was cradled in someone's lap and a gentle hand stroked my hair. I blinked again and found myself looking into a pair of very concerned blue eyes. "Jason?" I whispered as my jaw began to tremble. Someone had hit me! A shiver spread through my body and I realized how brutally cold it was lying on the wet ground. I struggled to force myself upwards but I needn't have fought because the arms around me readily helped.

"I'm not sure you should be standing," said Jason as I scrambled to get onto my feet. The world spun and I blinked, sinking gratefully against Jason.

"The police will be here any minute," said the other voice I heard. The realtor. What was she doing out here?

No, the more important question was: what was Jason doing here?

"Are you okay? What happened?" Gwendolyn asked, concern lacing her voice. "I heard someone scream and when Jason and I rushed outside, we saw someone running away."

"That's when we found you," added Jason. "Did someone hurt you?"

"I saw someone trying the door handle," I told them. I reached my hand to my head, relieved to find I wasn't bleeding although I fully expected to see a colorful bruise in the morning. "I think I surprised them and they rushed me and knocked me down."

"Them?"

"He," I clarified as my head began to throb, "Or she. I'm not sure. It happened so quickly. I screamed and they hit me. I must have been knocked out or passed out when I hit the floor."

Gwendolyn gasped and Jason tightened his arm around me. "Trouble seems to follow you around," he said softly but not at all accusingly. I was saved from giving him a tart answer by the blare of a police siren getting closer. Then a car screeched to a stop and multiple doors slammed.

"Detective Logan," called Jason. He lifted one hand in a wave.

"What the hell happened?" yelled Detective Logan as he crossed the lot, the beam from his flashlight dancing on the ground. "I got a call saying a woman had been attacked."

I raised a hand weakly. "That would be me."

"Someone was trying to break into one of the houses," the realtor told him, "I don't know why. I'm Gwendolyn Cooper, the realtor. There's nothing in there. This poor lady saw him and he hit her."

"He? You got a look at him?" Detective Logan squinted at me. I recoiled as the flashlight shone on my face.

I shook my head. "It was too dark and too unexpected."

"Why were you two out here?" he asked, dropping the light.

"I came to see the show home," I told him. "I heard it was really nice and I thought I would take a short walk before driving home."

"A short walk?" Detective Logan gave me a skeptical look. "In the dark? On a construction site?"

"I didn't say it was a good idea!" I muttered.

"Are you hurt?"

"No, I don't think so. My head hurts a little but I'll be okay."

Detective Logan turned his attention to Jason. "Did you see the person?"

"No."

"Were you two taking a walk together?"

"No!" we both chorused at the same time.

"Uh-huh," said Detective Logan slowly, clearly and unconvinced. "Sara, I think we should get your head looked at, just to be sure."

"I'm okay, really," I assured him.

He assessed me for a long moment before nodding. "At least come down to the station. The new recruit used to be an EMT and he can give you a swift check-up. Plus, I have a slightly ulterior motive. I'd like you to take a look at some photos."

The suggestion of photos lured me in without protest, just like I was sure Detective Logan knew it would, and I instantly agreed. Plus, if I were being honest too, having an EMT check my head and confirm it was nothing would give me some much-needed peace of mind.

"I'll follow you there," I told him.

"No way," said Jason and Detective Logan at the same time. They hesitated, looking at one another, then Logan took the lead.

"I think it's better if you ride with me," he said.

"I can follow in your car and pick up mine later," offered Jason.

"Why don't I arrange for your car to be taken to your home?" suggested Gwendolyn. I saw her worried grimace as she wrung her hands. "I'm sure you shouldn't be driving later and it's the least I can do, especially after you were injured here. It's not any trouble."

I nodded, grateful. "That would be really helpful, thank you."

"I'll follow you to the station and take you home after," added Jason.

"That sounds like a good plan," agreed Detective Logan, "You should probably take a look at the photos too. Maybe you'll recognize someone."

After I gave my car keys to Gwendolyn and she copied down my address, I got into the front of the squad car with Detective Logan. We were silent on the way to the station but every so often, I noted him taking a look in his rear mirror, checking to see if Jason still followed. I knew that was what he was doing because I was doing it too.

"How well do you know that guy?" asked Detective Logan when we turned into town.

"Jason? I met him a few weeks ago when he first came to town. I know him professionally better than personally," I said, then frowned. *Did I?* Before Jason had given me a ride into town, that would have been true; but now, after his kiss, I wasn't so sure.

"I had concerns about him after your friend was killed so I looked into him. He appears to be everything he claims to be."

"That's reassuring."

Detective Logan darted a glance at me and I thought I saw him smile in the dark. "I thought you might like to know."

"I'm glad you told me. If you hadn't, I might have really worried about why he was at the housing development tonight."

"He didn't say?"

"No."

"Huh. What were you really doing there?"

I knew that question was looming and at some point I would have to come up with a really good answer. As I hesitated, I thought about lying but figured that wouldn't help at all. "My mother said someone mentioned seeing Bree there. I thought it was strange, so I wanted to go check it out."

"You didn't think of mentioning it to me?"

"I wasn't planning on going out there. I just thought about it and kind of ended up there. I was taking a look around when I saw someone trying to break into the house."

"You figured Bree hid her loot there?"

"No! Well, yes, but I wasn't looking for it exactly. I don't care about the stupid jewels. I was just curious."

"It seems to me like someone else was too. Can you think of anyone else who knew about Bree's visit there?"

I shrugged. There was so much gossip flying around. "Anyone could have known."

"Damn!" Detective Logan hit the steering wheel with his open palm. "I hoped you weren't going to say that."

We fell into silence again, only speaking when we pulled up in front of the station. A moment later, Jason's car slid in behind it. We all got out and walked into the station together. Detective Logan had the new officer shine a light into my eyes, and do simple tests like following his finger with my eyes, and he also examined my head under a good light. He declared me absolutely fine with the possibility of a nasty bruise in the morning.

"Can I get either of you a hot drink?" asked Detective Logan. "It's the bump-on-the-head special treatment."

I laughed, the somber mood suddenly lifting, and declined. Jason, who followed us in, requested a coffee and Detective Logan sent one of the junior officers to fetch two cups. As we waited, he laid out a selection of photos on his desk. "I've been conferring with other police departments while looking into any suspected associates of Bree and these people are generally considered persons of interest. Take a look and let me know if any of them look familiar."

I started with the top column, carefully examining each face, knowing it was fruitless. I hadn't seen anyone in the library the night Bree was killed and it was too dark to see a face tonight. None of them triggered a memory. As I moved to the second row, Detective Logan said, "Perhaps you saw one or more around town before Bree was killed. Maybe you saw them speaking to her? Or parked outside the library?"

Moving to the end of the row, I shook my head, and continued to the third row. I stopped at the second photo. A woman looked familiar. In the photo, she had bangs and a blunt haircut, but I had seen her face before. I imagined the face without bangs and added lighter hair. "I know her," I said, pleased with myself. "This is Bree's sister, Angela Daniels. She called me yesterday and I met her earlier today when she got into town."

"Bree's sister?"

"Yeah, she looks different here but it's definitely her. She said you've been really helpful." I started to move on to look at the other photos but Detective Logan's next words stopped me.

"Bree didn't have a sister."

"Yes, she did. I met her."

"We looked into it, Sara. She doesn't."

"She said she spoke to you..." I trailed off at Detective Logan's pointed look.

"I haven't spoken to any member of Bree's family. As far as I can ascertain, she didn't have anyone and certainly, no siblings. As for this woman, her name isn't Angela Daniels. It's Angie Ackler."

"Then who..." I gulped as the implication became crystal clear. Angela wanted me to think she was Bree's sister, and she could only want that if she needed information about Bree from me.

"Did you tell her Bree was seen at the housing development?" Detective Logan inquired.

I thought back. "She was interested in all the places where Bree went around town and... oh, no! I *did* mention Bree was seen there."

"Could she have been around the same height as your attacker?"

"I'm not sure. Maybe. I thought it was a guy but I guess it could have been her." I clapped a hand over my mouth as the realization of how much danger I was in became apparent. "She told me she was staying at a motel out of town."

"Write down the name and address." Detective Logan got up and walked around the desk. With the notepad in hand, he leaned out of his office and called over two officers. He spoke to them quickly and they nodded, and jogged out of the small room with the address I'd written. "They're going to pick her up if she's still there."

"Who is she?" asked Jason. He'd been quiet all this time but I noted the anxiety in his voice.

"A suspected member of the same crew Bree worked with. Her fingerprints were picked up at one crime scene and her face turned up in security footage several times in the days before another one. We think she cases potential places and perhaps operates in some other capacity, like distraction. If she knows about the jewels, then she could have been in on Bree's final job."

"She thought I could lead her to the jewels," I realized. "How could I have been so stupid!"

"She probably took the information you gave her and used it to check out the housing development."

"If she thought about it seriously, she'd have to know that Bree couldn't have hidden the jewels in any empty properties," I said.

Jason frowned. "What do you mean?"

"I mean, the four almost finished houses might not have any residents yet but any number of contractors continue to work inside them. Bree wouldn't hide a stash that big in a place where they could be so easily discovered. Plus, she couldn't bury them on the land anywhere because they could get dug up, found, or lost. It would be too big a risk." Detective Logan and Jason both stared at me but I carried on. "I figured the only place Bree would hide the jewels if, and it's a big if, she intended to hide them there, would be on the one finished property. The show home. She could be almost certain that the house would be left alone since it's fully fitted out. She could walk in any time she liked."

"I'm impressed," said Detective Logan. "You've really thought a lot about this."

"It makes sense to me."

"Me too," he said, rising for a second time and waving a hand to the last remaining officer at his desk. Within minutes, he was also jogging out the door, armed with Detective Logan's instructions. "I'm going to take a look at the show home again. You don't recognize any other photos?"

I took another look, scanning each one. "No," I said.

"Okay. Can I trust you to go home and not investigate anything else?"

"Yes," I said with absolute certainty.

"I will walk Sara to her door and make sure she goes inside," said Jason.

"And I promise not to escape out the back," I added, trying not to smile.

"You make sure you don't do that," said Detective Logan. "We're all out of officers to respond tonight thanks to the new leads you've provided us with."

"Glad to be of help."

"Any point in asking you to stop helping?"

"I really will try," I said, which probably wasn't the answer he was looking for but the best and most honest one I had. Detective Logan opened his mouth, as if to tell me to try harder, then shut it again and shook his head.

"I'll walk you both out," he said after a long pause. He grabbed his jacket from where he draped it around the back of the chair and shrugged it on.

"I hope you catch her," I said as we walked out. "I can't believe I fell for all her lies. She seemed so upset about Bree."

"Don't beat yourself up about it. She's a professional, just like Bree."

I winced, his comment hitting the mark even if I thought he didn't mean to be so harsh. But Detective Logan was right, Bree was a professional liar and managed to sucker me a hundred percent. Now, with

Angela's appearance, it seemed more likely than ever that she must've double-crossed her gang, so it shouldn't have been any surprise that those people would come sniffing around eventually.

"I feel like an idiot," I told Jason as we got into his car.

"Why?"

I pointed to my bruised forehead instead of replaying the night's events. "At least Detective Logan didn't rub it in too much," I said, "but he's right, I should have told him sooner but I believed her. She seemed so sad."

"It just goes to show what a nice person you are," said Jason.

I turned to him. "You think?"

"Sure. You see the best in people. She gave you a grieving family member, exactly what you expected. Detective Logan said she was a professional." Jason hesitated.

"What is it?"

"You're just lucky she only wanted information."

"Yeah," I huffed, "I gave her exactly what she wanted." I paused, replaying the events in my mind again, knowing I would probably do so again that night. Something else occurred to me. "What were you doing there?"

"Where?"

"The housing development?"

"Oh. It's on my way and I thought I'd take a look."

"But the realtor called you by name."

"Did she?" Jason shrugged. "Here we are," he said, stopping almost outside my house. My car, as promised, had already been dropped off. I made a mental note to thank Gwendolyn for kindly arranging it although I suspected her eager goodwill had a lot to do with not getting the construction firm sued or losing her job.

"Thanks," I said. "I appreciate the lift."

"Take it easy tonight. I'll check in on you in the morning and if you need anything, don't hesitate to call," he said, making to reach for the handle.

"Oh, no, don't get out. It's too cold and I'm sure you want to get home, I mean, to your hotel," I told him, resting my arm on his to stop him. I thanked him again, promised I would call if I needed anything, and hurried to my house. Jason waited until I opened the door and waved but he didn't leave until I closed the door. I watched his tail lights from my living room window, waiting until he turned the corner.

There was a lot to contemplate and I almost wished I was officially involved. I was dying to find out whether they found Bree's fake sister tonight or any traces of the person who pushed me over at the construction site. I thought about calling but figured Detective Logan wouldn't appreciate it. I was sure the only thing that saved me from his wrath tonight was the bump on my head. I hoped that he would have some good news in the morning.

One thing was very clear to me: just like Bree, Jason had definitely been to the construction site before, but why?

CHAPTER TWENTY

My phone buzzed in my pocket. I reached for it, checked the screen and replaced it. That was Jason's second text and the second one I chose to ignore. I wasn't quite sure how to reply to his friendly inquiry about my head this morning. The questions of why he was at the development, and managed to arrive exactly when I got knocked down, continued to echo in my head and I couldn't come up with a good conclusion.

Detective Logan's warning about trusting people had also shaken me. I blindly trusted the fake sister and she used me. I'd also come to trust Jason, but was he using me too? Detective Logan said he checked him out and he was fine but was that enough? It wasn't the first time Jason had suddenly arrived on the scene when I'd been hurt or in need of help. Was it all a big ploy? Was he trying to make me trust him before he revealed his desire to find Bree's loot too? I felt horrible for thinking so but

I couldn't help it. Yesterday's events made me more than a little suspicious.

Unfortunately, I had something more pressing to think about now.

"Sara?"

"Hmm?" I didn't realize Detective Logan was speaking until he said my name.

"I said, it looks like someone did try to force open the window," said Detective Logan. "There're tool marks on the outside and it's quite possible they tried another window further along too. My guess is they tried to pick the lock but the door held fast so they went around back and tried to open all the windows."

"It doesn't look like they got in though," I said.

"I think they got scared off after they smashed a pane. I patched it up as best I could. There's a lot of public interest in the library right now and no telling how many people were sneaking around throughout the night."

I shivered. "That gives me the creeps."

"The rain washed away any prints so there's not much I can do, other than just file a report and give you a general warning. Make sure all windows and doors are locked when you leave. Is there anyone who can stay with you until you finish locking up?"

Just as I was trying to decide who might have been available, I got his implication. "You think someone would have the gall to try and force their way in when I'm locking up?"

"I hope not, but it's not unheard of. Would you consider shutting the library down? Just for a few days? I can speak to your boss if it's an issue."

I shook my head, knowing that wasn't possible. Any hint of forcing a closure would mean the library almost certainly wouldn't open again. Plus, I had to take advantage of the upsurge in interest if I intended to gather anymore signatures for the petition. "You know how the council feels about it; they want to shut the library. I don't have too long before it closes for good. If I close it up now, I doubt it will ever reopen."

"Could that possibly be a good thing?" asked Detective Logan.

"Not if we want to keep this library!" I offered the petition to him. "Can the town and I count on your support?"

"Already signed it," said Logan. "Okay, well, since you're probably the most stubborn person in town this week, can you at least think about changing your closing time? Your routine is too well known. I don't think opening should be a problem since there are plenty of people around, even in winter; but at closing, it's dark and most people have already gone home. If I intended to bully my way past you, that's when I'd do it."

"I agree. How about if I close up fifteen minutes earlier?" I replied.

"Fine. I know you haven't asked me, but I'm sure you want to, although I don't think this news will make you happy at all. We didn't find any clues at the construction site. Gwendolyn Cooper didn't see anything more than a fleeing figure and a dark car. Jason Rees only saw the flash of a tail light."

"I guessed that might be the case. What about Bree's fake sister?"

Detective Logan shook his head. "She was already gone. I'm not sure she even registered at the motel she told you about. It was probably just another lie. She might have pumped you for information, passed it on to a contact and left town; or she might be hiding out somewhere closeby, getting ready to try again. She might even try and contact you again."

"Do you think so?"

"It's a definite possibility. She can't be sure we've spoken unless she's watching one of us, so she might think it's safe to try again. My money, however, is on her not making another approach. She wouldn't want to arouse your suspicion."

"Who me?" I laughed, but it was hollow and my smile didn't match my eyes. The idea of being targeted, watched, and carefully interrogated made me incredibly uneasy. With Detective Logan's warning that someone might try to break into the library again, I was sure my uneasiness would not subside.

"Take care," said Detective Logan. "I wish I could get this thing wrapped up faster but this case is a helluva lot bigger than Calendar."

I waved to him as he left, my phone already buzzing again. I checked it and saw another text from Jason. This time, I tapped out a short reply. *At work. Feeling okay. Thanks for checking in on me,* and hit send, hoping that would suffice. There wasn't anything else to say and I didn't want to feel that he, too, was drilling me for information. That would have been too disappointing. I trusted Bree and she let me down. I hadn't even liked Jason at the start but in the past few days, he was good company. After the kiss, I even allowed myself to daydream about dating him in an ideal world, one where he wasn't trying to bulldoze my favorite town landmark. An undeniable attraction to him had been brewing in my head even before we kissed. Now, with my newly suspicious thoughts, I was conflicted. What if Jason were only cozying up to me to get to the jewels too? That could explain his Knight in Shining Armor act.

However, I shouldn't have been thinking about another man when I'd already gone out with Tom and agreed to another date. At least Tom wasn't conveniently appearing every time danger popped up. Actually, we hadn't even spoken yesterday like we said we would. I swallowed the guilty feeling that my preoccupation with Jason meant Tom hadn't even popped into my head until now.

Back at my desk, I toyed with my phone. I had only just opened the library for the day when I immediately had to call the police at the discovery of the attempted break-in. So I hadn't yet started any work. Instead, I took a few moments to ponder the idea of calling Tom and suggesting we meet for lunch or supper. I hoped that would get my mind off other things, *especially Jason.*

Before I even got the opportunity to make the call, the middle school children I'd been expecting trooped in, all chatter and giggles. I plastered a broad smile on my face and swiftly moved into true librarian mode, inviting them to take seats on the carpet in the children's area. I was well prepared to begin the talk they expected. At the end, I handed out tasks to them. They had to find certain books relating to their class topic on the world. As they hurried away in pairs to locate the appropriate books, their teacher came to join me.

"I can't believe this won't be here much longer," she said. "I love coming here and so do the children."

"We're still collecting more signatures," I told her.

"I signed already. Do you think there will be enough?"

"I only need a hundred more to reach the target. That will only be enough to make the council listen; it won't necessarily sway them. I'm not sure what else I can do."

"What if the children all wrote letters saying how important the library is to them?"

"You would do that?" I beamed at her thoughtful suggestion.

"Absolutely!"

By the time they trooped out, I was feeling more upbeat. Petition signatures were one thing, but reading how important the library was to children took it to another level of emotion that I never considered. Leaving a few browsers downstairs, I went up to the second floor, moving over to one of the displays I created about the town. Many of those residents wouldn't still be alive now; but I wondered if I had enough time to track down their descendants. If I could do that, perhaps they would write letters to the council too?

Aubrey, who usually worked Saturdays but kindly volunteered to cover some of Bree's hours, came in at noon. I gave her a quick update on the plan for the day and told her I was taking my lunch in the office. I ate my sandwiches at my desk, like I often did, and mulled over the previous day's events again. When I realized I was doing little more than giving myself a headache, I pushed the thoughts to one side and reached for my phone.

Tom picked up on the fourth ring. "Hello, stranger," he said. "I was just thinking about you. You must have read my mind."

"It's my secret super power," I teased, happy to hear his voice.

"Do you have any other secret powers?"

"Yes. Persuasion."

"Okay, I'll bite. Persuade me of something."

"Let's meet for a drink later," I said, emboldened.

"Yes," he said quickly. "Wow! Would you look at that? Your powers really do work! When should I pick you up?"

"Seven," I told him.

"It's a date."

~

I brushed on a layer of lipstick and pouted in the mirror. I didn't wear a lot of makeup usually but I felt like making a special effort for our date and was rather pleased with the results. The bruise was fully covered with a blend of concealer and foundation, my cheeks were delicately blushed, my lashes were thick and long, and the lipstick was just the right shade of pink: not Barbie, not vampy, but a delicate, rosy hue.

Closing the lid, I slipped the lipstick into my purse just as a knock sounded at my door. I hurried downstairs and opened it, glad I'd already pulled on my knee-length boots.

"You look so beautiful," said Tom, leaning in to kiss me, first one cheek and then the other. "I hope I'm not late. I think I took a wrong turn and ended up in a cul-de-sac a couple of streets away."

"I know the one. It has a similar name to this road and people often go the wrong way."

"Fortunately, I know someone who knows their way to the bar so I think we'll make it there without any problems," he said. "Ready to go?"

I reached for my jacket, wrapping it around me and grabbed my purse. "Ready!"

Tom kept up a steady chatter as we drove, and I found myself enjoying him. I liked to just listen to him talk. He told me about his job in advertising sales, why he was in Calendar, and how it was changing his opinion of small towns. He even said he thought he could settle down somewhere like this, especially since he could run his business from home. It heartened me to hear that he liked my town so much that he was considering sticking around. Otherwise, a third date might have been right out of the question! It is pretty hard to date someone long distance.

We took up seats at the bar and ordered beers, shrugging off our jackets and looking around at the occupied pool tables. I waved to my friend, Meredith, who sat at a table with a man I didn't recognize. Then I saw my friend, Rachel, and her sister in a corner booth, but they were engrossed in conversation. The music was just right and we could speak over it without shouting. I figured there would be dancing later. On our second bottles of beer, Tom insisted on ordering a few snacks and the barman returned with them, spreading the little dishes between us.

"I enjoyed our dinner," Tom said as he looked over toward the pool table, "but I like this too. I'm not sure I remember the last time I played a game of pool. Do you play?"

"I do, but I'm not great," I admitted.

"Hmm, I'm not sure I buy that." He winked at me. "Is this one of those times where you say you're not great and then you slay me on our first game?"

I laughed, shaking my head and letting my hair tumble around my shoulders. Tom reached over and brushed a lock back and our eyes met. I began to lean in for the inevitable kiss, blinking in surprise when Tom jumped to the floor. "Luck is on our side tonight!" he exclaimed, inclining his head to the pool table. "Let's play."

"You're on," I agreed, shaking myself. Apparently, Tom never had a clue I thought he was about to kiss me.

Tom set up the balls and handed me a pool cue. "Do you want to break?" he asked.

"No, you go ahead."

"Hmmm, I have a feeling you're just being nice because you intend to annihilate me," he said, bending to position his cue. After a moment, he straightened up again. "Why don't we make this more interesting?" he suggested. "You win, you buy the next round of drinks. I win, I take you to dinner."

"That doesn't seem fair," I started to protest. "The bet should be equal."

"Fine. You win, you can take me to dinner. Not at a drive-through, either," he warned, laughing. He pushed up his sleeves and stretched out his arm. I glanced at the balls, waiting for the inevitable crack that told me they'd been struck. It was followed by him lining the cue up until it rested between his thumb and forefinger. His wristwatch glinted under the bar's overhead lights and I frowned. A dark mark spread from under the watch, coiling around his wrist. No, not a mark. A tattoo.

The ink wasn't a coil, but a tail that curved around to the underside of his wrist. Pincers spread out on either side of the clock-face and curved inward. Even without seeing the rest of the scorpion tattoo, I knew what the pincers held. A diamond.

I stepped closer, my heart thumping as I recalled where I'd seen a similar tattoo before.

It was the tattoo on the man Bree ripped out of her photo.

Cold fear washed through me and I stumbled, gripping the side of the table just as the cueball hit, causing the others to fly apart, ricocheting against each other. In an instant, Tom was at my side. "Are you okay?" he asked, concern etched across his face.

"I caught my heel," I lied quickly. Blood drained from my face. "I thought I was going to fall."

Tom hooked an arm around my waist and kissed the top of my head. The gesture should have been reassuring. Instead, I felt sick. "I've got you," he said.

"Will you excuse me? I need to go to the restroom," I told him.

"Sure. I promise not to move any of the balls until you're back." He smiled his brilliant, white smile but this time, I couldn't see it reflected in his face. The ready smile, I realized, had never reached his eyes.

"Great!" I grinned, walking as quickly as I could to the restrooms near the back of the bar. I hurried inside, pushing the door shut and resting my back against it as I breathed hard, feeling hopelessly trapped with no escape.

Not only was I on a date with Bree's pyscho ex, but he was also my ride and I had no other way home! I couldn't call a taxi because he would see me leave and I couldn't insist he drive me home without possibly alerting him something was wrong. I could fake my way through the date but I wasn't sure how long I could keep it up. I wasn't a practiced liar or a criminal. Tom was. Tom read people for a living.

"That bad, huh?" said a voice.

I jumped. I hadn't realized I wasn't alone. "Sorry?" I said, noticing the blonde woman in the mirrors, adjusting the collar of a pale pink blouse. I could only smile in relief. "Meredith?" I sighed. "I am so glad to see you!"

"Me too. I am on the worst date. The first date I've had in... I don't know how long. I never should have come," she confided as she pulled a face. "I never realized how offensive he was because I never spoke to him any length of time before. I think he hates women."

"So... not a keeper?" I asked, my heart rate slowing as my panic lessened.

She wavered her head from side to side. "I'm thinking no. In fact, he is the prime example of why I don't date. What's wrong with your date?"

"I think he might be psycho."

Meredith's eyes widened. "Damn!"

"I need to get out of here and I don't want to get into a car with him. He picked me up and drove us here," I told her in a rush.

"I'm parked outside but I need a low key exit," said Meredith. "We need a ruse. How about you going back to the pool table and I'll call you from the restroom. You can pretend your mom has been in an accident and you need to leave at once. I'll offer to run you over there. In fact, I'll insist on it."

"You would do that?"

"In the name of sisterhood and getting out of this date? Yes! A million times."

"Okay," I agreed. "What if he realizes I'm lying?"

"You think he'd get nasty?"

"I don't know, maybe."

"Better make it believable then," said Meredith. "Ready?"

I nodded quickly, knowing if I thought about it any longer, I would probably risk running out the doors and hoping Tom didn't catch me. For the first time that day, I wished Jason were there to rescue me again. "Give me ten seconds," I said. "I left my purse on the pool table."

Meredith gave me a nod and readied her phone. I took a deep breath, smoothed my skirt, and walked out of the restroom, forcing myself to smile as soon as I saw Tom. When I got back to the pool table, my phone began to vibrate in my purse. I reached for it. "Excuse me a moment," I said, shielding the screen from his view. "Hello?"

"Say hi mom," said Meredith. I scanned the bar for her but couldn't see her.

"Hi, Mom. I'm out on a date right now. Is everything okay?"

"Blah blah hospital," said Meredith.

I clasped a hand to my mouth, frowning hard. "Oh, my gosh! What happened?"

"Blah blah more stuff about hospitals."

"That sounds terrible. Are you hurt? Of course I'll come right away. No, it's no trouble, really," I said. "I'll get there as soon as I can."

"Great. We're out of here," said Meredith and she hung up.

"Is something wrong?" asked Tom.

"It's my mom. There's been a..." I stopped, hearing my name being called. I turned around, seeing Meredith hurrying towards me, waving.

"I just got a call from my dad," she said, reaching for my hands, her face furrowed with panic. "He said your mom has been in some kind of accident with my mom. I told him I knew where you were and we'd leave right away."

"I just heard," I said, hoping I looked as stunned as I felt.

"We have to go," she said, hooking her arm through mine.

"I'll drive you," said Tom, tossing his pool cue onto the table.

"No need to," said Meredith. "My car is right outside and I can drive us both. We have to hurry." She began to propel us toward the door before Tom could protest while I tucked my purse under my arm, and we traipsed through the parking lot. We ran to her car and threw ourselves inside, Meredith laughing.

"You are quite the actress," I told her, impressed.

"Thank you. You know what?" she asked.

I shook my head. "What?"

"I was so busy helping you get out of your date, I forgot to tell mine I was leaving. He probably still thinks I'm in the restroom! What the hell! Let's get out of here." We pulled out of the lot and Meredith accelerated. "What makes you think he's psycho?" she asked. "Was he the date you bought that awesome dress for?"

"Yes, and I still love it, but I realized he wasn't who he said he was," I replied.

She shot a worried look at me. "He was lying? What about?"

"I'm not sure, but I think probably everything."

"Wow. Married? Kids?"

"No idea. I hope not."

"Well, whatever he is, you're out of there now. Do you want to go somewhere else and talk about it?"

"If you don't mind, I think I'd like to go home." I didn't add, *and call Detective Logan.*

"No problem, but we should go out for lunch sometime. Not with creepy guys."

Meredith had always been friendly but had never suggested a social occasion before. Despite my worries, I was pleased at her overture. "I'd like that."

"I promise not to fake an accident to leave either," she said and we both laughed.

I didn't feel a lot better by the time Meredith dropped my off at my house. I wasn't even sure I should have gone home at all. Tom knew where I lived and I didn't want him to drive by and see I was home rather than at my mom's, per my fake story, nor did I want him knocking on the door, or worse!

My mind made up, I hurried into my bedroom and grabbed a couple of changes of clothes, throwing them into an overnight bag and adding my toiletries. As I locked up my house, I sent my mother a text message saying I was on my way and I needed to stay the night.

Next, I called Detective Logan. The phone rang and rang before his answer service clicked on. "I saw him," I said, "I mean, it's Sara Cutler. I think I know who Bree's ex-boyfriend is, the one that she betrayed. He's in town. I think he's been trying to get information from me to find out where... oh..." I stopped and clapped a hand over my mouth. How could I have been so blind? I knew where the jewels were! I'd known all along. They had been right in front of me the whole time and if I were right, they were only steps away from where Bree was killed. My mind raced. Tom must have threatened her for them and she didn't tell him where they were despite their close proximity. "I know where the jewels are," I said into the phone. "They're at the library. I'm going to get them, and then I'm coming to the station."

I hung up and started the engine of my cold car before backing out of my driveway. I drove to the library, parking outside. It would take only minutes to hurry inside and get Bree's jewels, and I could make sure Detective Logan had them and returned them to their rightful owners.

I pulled the keys from my pocket and climbed out, hurrying along the dark path toward the door. I fumbled with the old lock, but got the key in and twisted, pushing the door open just as something hard pressed against my back.

"About time," said a deep voice.

CHAPTER TWENTY-ONE

Ice-cold dread filled me. Frozen to the spot, I was unable to move, even though the door stood ajar. Thoughts filled my head. A few years ago, I enrolled in a self-defense course. If I could power myself backwards, I could inflict some serious injury on my opponent, and with him disadvantaged, I could run for help. Immediately, I knew that wouldn't work. He would shoot me the moment I pushed backward and there was no way I could get the gun moved away from the small of my back. If I could manage to get out of this, I decided I would have to complain to the self-defense instructor for not covering such an issue.

If I stepped forwards fast enough, I could grab the heavy door and slam it in his face. Only... there was that same little problem of him shooting me first. Plus, if he pushed the door back, it seemed more likely that he would send me sprawling as he closed the door behind him, trapping us inside. There was no way I wanted to be injured and stuck inside the empty library with him.

Another thought struck me: he could only be here because, like me, he thought the jewels were hidden in the library.

"Inside," said Tom, nudging me again with the gun.

"Detective Logan knows where I am," I replied, not moving as I stalled for time. All I needed was enough time for Detective Logan to get my message.

"Sure he does," said Tom, his voice suddenly scathing. He pushed harder and I stumbled forwards, all hope ebbing out of me. Behind us, the door shut with a bang. I reached for the lights like I normally would but Tom batted my hand away. "No lights," he hissed. "Lights on at this time would alert people, wouldn't it? Keep your hands up and don't try anything else stupid."

"I won't," I whispered, my heart racing.

"Go get them."

"Get what?" I asked, even though I knew exactly what he meant.

"What did I say about not doing anything stupid? You know exactly what I'm talking about."

I thought about Meredith's words regarding acting and I knew I had to keep up the pretense. Tom couldn't possibly be sure that I already figured out where Bree had stashed the jewels—in plain sight—and he couldn't be sure they were here either. Otherwise, he would have tried to retrieve them before. With a heavy sigh, I realized he had been here before, probably several times. Tom must have tried to convince Bree to reveal the jewels' whereabouts and she hadn't told him. Yet he'd also been here the night of the party, free to wander wherever he pleased, and it must have been him who tried to break in through the now boarded-up window. What he really needed was me. With a crushing realization, I knew that his attention was all an act. He played me the whole time. I had to play him right back. I had to keep up my charade and convince him that I didn't know what he was talking about until Detective Logan arrived to save me.

I just hoped he wouldn't be too late.

"The jewels," Tom continued. "Tell me where the jewels are, Sara, or I'll be forced to use this."

"I don't believe you," I said, realizing how ridiculous I sounded. Of course Tom would use it! He already shot Bree dead and he knew her. He wouldn't hesitate to shoot me.

"Turn around."

I turned around slowly, my hands still in the air, not quite above my head in surrender, but high enough that it felt like I was pushing the air between us.

Tom didn't look any different from our date and I decided he must have left the bar soon after I did, perhaps coming straight here to lie in wait for me. Only his express had changed. Despite my best efforts at acting, he obviously didn't believe my excuse. "Do you think I bought that ruse about your mom?" he asked, confirming my suspicions and wagging a finger at me. "You nearly got me. You looked worried but it was too much of a coincidence that your friend's parents were involved too. Her date might have bought it, but I didn't. All it took was one phone call to confirm that your mom hadn't moved from her living room all night. Apparently, she's having a lot of fun this evening with her friends."

"You're watching my mom?" I felt sick at the thought.

"I'm not but my associate is. I think you met her already."

"Bree's fake sister?" I guessed.

Tom nodded. "She's sitting right outside your mom's house. One word from me, and your mom is going to have the worst night of her life."

Fear struck me like a slap. "You wouldn't dare!"

"You know I would. See? I have it all figured out, Sara. We both know it'll be a lot easier if you just tell me where the jewels are. I know now Brittany hid them in the library somewhere but she was stupid enough not to tell me where; and look what happened to her."

"You killed her."

Tom shrugged. "It was her own fault. All she had to do was hand them over. Even better, she shouldn't have double-crossed me in the first place; so really, she had it coming." A shard of moonlight lit up his face. For the first time, I noticed the hard, angular lines and the unpleasant set of his jaw. Had he always looked like this? Or was I only now truly seeing him for the first time? "You are not going to be that idiotic," he told me.

"What makes you think I know where the jewels are? If I knew, wouldn't I have found them already?"

"I don't think so. I think you were as clueless as everyone else at the start. It's been kind of funny actually, watching that detective bumbling around, trying to work everything out. Then, all the town crazies came out with their spades and shovels and started digging the place up!" Tom laughed.

Much as I didn't want to, I couldn't disagree with the last part. The promise of a treasure trove was as contagious as a scarlet fever to the Calendar residents, making them all a little crazy. It also attracted a much worse kind of crazy but I didn't plan to tell Tom that. Not while he had a gun pointed at me.

"I've done a little digging around about you. Everyone says nice things about you, you know? Sara Cutler is so *nice*. Sara is *such* a good friend. Sara is *so* honest. Sara is so *perfect*," he sneered. "I figured if you knew where the jewels were, you would have turned them over to Detective Logan by now."

"That's right, I would have," I agreed. "But since I haven't..." I stopped, hoping he came to the conclusion that I still didn't know.

"You want to know what I think? I think you didn't know," said Tom, not waiting for an answer. "I followed you into the city with that guy and I wondered if you managed to track down someone from Brittany's past. I couldn't be sure, but you didn't seem to know anything on our date. I even asked you about hiding places at the party and you were oblivious. I think somehow, you managed to figure it out tonight. I've run our conversation through my head, and I can't figure out how but somehow, you realized who I was and where the jewels were. It's time to confess." He raised the gun, leveling it with my forehead.

"You're right. I did figure out you were Bree's ex," I told him, raising my hands a little higher, terrified that he would shoot me. "I saw the tattoo on your wrist, the one under your watch, when you pushed your sleeves up. I recognized it from a photo Bree had and that's why

I made up the story about my mom being in an accident. But I swear, I don't know where the jewels are! Please! You have to believe me!"

Disappointment flashed across his face. "Then why are you here? There's no reason for you to be in the library at night."

I glanced around, looking for a reason and quickly spied my desk. "I needed to pick up the petitions to take to my boss first thing tomorrow morning," I lied.

"And you decided to come now? I don't buy it." Tom squeezed the trigger. As I ducked, a squeal erupting from my throat, the wall splintered behind my head. I dropped to the floor, covering my head, waiting for the inevitable bright light that told me I was crossing over. Except it didn't come. Instead, Tom shouted at me. "Get up!" he yelled. "That was a warning shot! Tell me where the jewels are or the next one hits you in the stomach. I can assure you, that's a long, slow, agonizing death. If that doesn't persuade you, then one call from me and your mother is next in line." He held up his phone, the screen blinking to life.

"I swear I don't know," I said, my voice wobbling. I edged to my feet, my whole body tensing as I waited any moment for the gun to fire.

"I really don't want to do this," said Tom. "But you leave me no other choice. Let's go upstairs. That's where Brittany went to get them."

"She told you she hid them in here?" I asked as he waved his gun, indicating I should go first. I sidestepped to my left, keeping my back to the wall, reluctantly turning away from him as we crossed the floor to the staircase. I took the steps slowly, wishing I could turn in a flash and high kick him across the room before racing to freedom. Unfortunately, I only read those stories about plucky heroines; I didn't star in them!

The library seemed ominous at night. The shelving cast shadows across the floor and even the stained-glass window barely allowed any light. I passed the slim beam it created, stumbling, and grabbed hold of the banister. I pulled myself up as Tom gave me a little push forwards. At the top of the steps, I paused, not wanting to go near the area of the room where Bree died. Unfortunately, Tom had other ideas. He planted a hand between my shoulder blades and propelled me forwards, his heavy footsteps behind me, almost masking the creak that came from below.

"It was tough tracking Bree down. She slipped away right after our last heist. I had to bribe a cop to trace her last cellphone usage, then I searched every town nearby until I got here. I found her almost by accident—" Tom laughed again, the sound chilling as he explained "—I literally saw her on the street. She looked so different. She changed her hair and how she dressed. I followed her around for a few days to make sure it was her; then I approached her when she left work. I don't know who was more shocked, she or I. I told her she needed to return what she stole and gave her an hour or I'd come back looking for her. By then, I knew where she lived and where she worked. I knew she'd try to double-cross me again, of course. That's just Bree's nature. She thought I left but I was still watching her. All I had to do was follow her back here. She waited for you to leave, then she let herself in. I slipped in behind her, following her as she went upstairs. She tried to insist she'd hidden them elsewhere. I got frustrated. I had to shoot her! Then you came back and I didn't have enough time to search. I actually thought I might have gotten it wrong, and that she really did stash them elsewhere. I knew I had to cozy up to you to find out more information about where that might be. You really took the bait when I suggested you look for them yourself. If you'd been a little faster, I wouldn't have had to plant a fake sister to gain your trust, but I was running out of time."

"That was you at the housing development? You hit me?" I asked, knowing it must be true.

"Yeah. You surprised me."

"And you tried to break into the library?"

"No, that was Angie. She thought she'd try her luck here while I was occupied. If she'd succeeded, we wouldn't be here now. I think Brittany came to get something from up here," he said. "You must've figured that out."

"She might have hidden something in one of the books," I lied, still stalling. *Where was Detective Logan?* "Some people hollow out the insides of books and hide things inside them. She might have done that."

Tom glanced at the racks spreading across the room. They contained thousands of books. There was no way of knowing which one could be a secret hiding place and I had to rely on that. "Start opening them," he said. "Don't bother to be neat. Just open them and toss them on the floor."

"It could take hours."

"I've waited this long."

"And what happens when I find them?" I asked, keeping my voice even.

"You've seen me," said Tom, a sad note in his tone. He took a deep breath, probably reminding himself of what was important. "I can't let you live."

A gun cocked. A flash of anger passed across Tom's face. "What did you do?" he yelled.

"It's not what she did, but what I'm going to do," said Detective Logan, his voice impossibly calm as he stepped off the staircase. His footsteps were lighter than I ever would have suspected. "Set your weapon on the floor, drop to your knees, and place your hands on top of your head. Sara, are you okay?"

"I'm fine," I told him, relief flooding me as soon as I saw Detective Logan stepping to the side of Tom. Behind him was Jason, his face stricken.

"Tom Nicholson, you're under arrest," started Detective Logan. He didn't get any further. Tom whirled around, firing a shot. Logan dropped to the floor, and fired back a single bullet. Tom wavered for a moment, then dropped to his knees, crying out. The gun fell to the floor as Tom clamped a hand over his shoulder, groaning.

Detective Logan rushed forwards, kicking Tom's gun to the side before restraining him.

"He has someone watching my mom," I told the detective.

With one knee in Tom's back, holding him down, Logan reached for his radio, dispatching officers to my mother's home, warning them of the waiting threat.

When the lights came on, flooding the library, I had to blink. I realized Jason was missing only when he hurried back, his footsteps louder as he took the stairs two at a time. He rushed past Detective Logan and a bleeding Tom, before wrapping his arms around me. "I heard everything," he said. "We both did."

I clung to him. "How did you know where I was?"

"I was in a meeting with Gwendolyn—the realtor at Bayview Drive—when Detective Logan came in. I overheard him getting your message and followed him here."

"Why? I mean, how? Actually, I mean why? You never told me why you were at Bayview last night. What were you doing with the realtor?" I asked, my words tumbling out in a mess.

"Last night, I was there because I was thinking about purchasing a house. I love the city but I've always wanted to be out in the country. I like Calendar. It's a great town. I could work in the city during the week and come out here on weekends. Maybe even get a dog like I always wanted. Plus," he said, taking my hands in his, "there's another reason for spending more time out here."

My heart sank. "So you can keep an eye on your new development?" I said.

Jason laughed. "No! Well, not this development, not anymore. I've been out to Bayview Drive a few times this week, looking at the plans, after I heard the developers ran into financial difficulties and were struggling to finish the homes there. I struck a deal with them. My firm is buying them out and finishing the construction. We don't need the library anymore. That's why I was talking to Gwendolyn. I came to deliver new plans and a new contract so she could work with us."

I was sure I had never looked more confused. "I don't understand. The library will just be bought be someone else."

Jason grinned. "I thought of that too. I went to the city to pitch a new section of the business to my firm. We're calling it town regeneration. The library will be our flagship project. To encourage towns to work with us, we'll offer to regenerate part of their town. Landscape a new park, build a new play area, make over the town library, that kind of thing." He paused, letting the information sink in.

"You saved my library?" I gasped.

Jason shook his head. "No. You did that. Your passion simply inspired me."

"Oh, shut up!" snarled Tom. "You two are making me sick!"

"You know what will really make you sick?" I told him, smiling now that I was safe and my mother was protected. "It's knowing that you were right. I did work out where Bree hid the jewels. They are here. But not up here."

"What are you talking about?" asked Detective Logan. Both he and Jason flashed me puzzled glances as Tom's face darkened.

"Wait just a moment," I said. I rushed downstairs, hurrying to my office where I pulled out a small container. I cranked open the lid, smiling when I saw what was inside. I hurried back to the waiting men. "Bree did stash the stolen jewels in Calendar but she didn't waste any time burying them or hiding them somewhere difficult that she might have had trouble accessing again. Instead, she hid them in plain sight. She was a master at creating beautiful dioramas in the display cases around the library and I had no problem leaving her to the task. Her last creation was a pirate theme. Pirate fiction, a treasure chest... only the jewels weren't paste or rhinestones." I held the plastic container out for them to see the sparkling jewels inside. Before the party, I scooped them up and stashed them away, forgetting about them almost instantly. I couldn't fathom how much they were worth. "She used real jewels for her displays of pirate treasure and starry skies."

"Unbelievable," muttered Detective Logan, shaking his head. "Tom Nicholson, did I mention you were under arrest not just for murder, but also for grand larceny?"

I smiled as Tom hung his head.

Outside, a police siren wailed.

CHAPTER TWENTY-TWO

"I was in terrible danger," said my mother, her hand flying to her throat as her enraptured audience gasped. Around her, the library books were abandoned in open boxes as my mother recounted her "ordeal" again. "The officer found the fiend waiting outside my home. There was a gun in her car! She was probably going to shoot me!"

"I don't think she was going to shoot you, Mom," I said. "She was just there to ensure my compliance with them."

"A gun, Sara. A gun! Imagine if you hadn't complied!"

I stepped away as my mother's friends leaned in, eager for more details. Not that she had anymore to give but I figured their conversation would run in a circular fashion for the next six weeks at least. Plus, I had to step away before I pointed out I *hadn't* complied with Tom's demands. I didn't think that nugget of information would have been very pleasing to my mother. Plus, I didn't want to hear that I'd risked her life for, oh, *the rest of my life!* Despite the good outcome, I still felt guilty that Tom and his associates had tried to drag my mother into their criminal business, using my fear for her safety and well-being to manipulate me.

"I can't believe we've done this much work," said Jaclyn, waving me over as she set up the cups on a large tray, ready to give to our thirsty helpers. Her leg was out of plaster but she was still moving quite slowly.

"I can't either," I agreed, looking around the library. We'd been hard at work all morning, packing the rarer books and storing them away, then packing the popular fiction and children's sections, stacking the boxes neatly to one side, and getting them ready to be moved into storage. Fortunately, a large amount of people volunteered to help so the packing had become less of a challenge and more of an enthusiastic party. Now all that remained were our core group: my mom, Jaclyn, Candice, Meredith, and the Rileys.

"It looks so much bigger now that it's empty," Jaclyn continued. "At least it's only for a couple of weeks."

With a pang, I realized that the library would have looked just like this if we were closing for good. Thankfully, that wasn't the case now. Jason had come through on his promise to regenerate the library as part of his firm's commitment to the towns where they planned to seek permits for new construction. Thanks to his rescue plan, we were only closing it for two weeks, long enough for the floors to be sanded and re-varnished, the walls and staircase to be given new coats of paint, and a new computer system to be installed, along with facilities for e-books and audiobooks. The funding also included windows to be replaced with energy-efficient ones and the roof would finally get repaired. In the springtime, the gardeners would be hired to give the garden a much-needed overhaul and install new seating areas. It was so exciting, I could hardly contain my enthusiasm.

"It's going to look so beautiful when we reopen," I told her. "I've already planned a grand celebration and a program of events that are designed to appeal to as many people as we can." I was even able to hire a new assistant to replace Bree after carefully making sure her work history was fully vetted. There would be no more horrible surprises at the library in the future, only good ones.

I poured coffees and teas and added a large plate of cookies, thanks to Jaclyn's donation, before taking them over to the desk—the last large piece of furniture that had yet to be moved—and waved everyone over. "I can't thank you enough for all your help," I told them as the volunteers gathered into a horseshoe shape. "It's amazing what we can all do when we join together..."

"Enough of that." Mrs. Riley waved a hand. "We want to know what's going on with the jewels. Did you really find them?"

"Yes, I did," I confirmed, "and I'm so pleased to see so many of you..."

"Did Bree really hide them in the library where everyone could see them?" asked Mr. Riley.

"She camouflaged them in one of the display cases," I replied. "Back to the library..."

"How much were they worth? Did you keep any?" asked my mother.

I gaped at my mother. "No, Mom! I didn't. Anyway, I..." I stopped, knowing it was futile. I should have guessed the turnout had something to do with the arrests that were made, and the recovery of the jewels. The headline of the *Calendar Times* had made darn sure it remained the hot topic.

"Fine, I'll tell you everything," I replied, figuring I might as well. "Bree walked into the library late last fall and asked about the job. I didn't have any other candidates and she seemed very nice and eager and her reference was good so I hired her. I know now that she made up her reference. Perhaps she had a friend helping her, or maybe she disguised her voice. I don't think I'll ever know for certain. Anyway, hiring her seemed like a really good decision. Bree was great. Super helpful, really creative and everyone liked her. I never had a single suspicion about her until the day I came back to the library and found her dead."

I stopped at the collective gasps and waited for the whispers to subside. "There was no reason for anyone to kill Bree that I knew of. There was also nothing to steal, or so we thought. In reality, Bree was killed just yards from where she'd stashed the jewels. Detective Logan thinks she refused to say where they were, hoping that her ex-boyfriend, Tom Nicholson, or Tricky as he's known in the criminal world, would spare her long enough for her to retrieve them and get away. She was overheard saying she planned to leave Calendar as soon as it was safe."

Meredith raised a hand. "I overheard that," she said to collective "oohs!"

"Imagine! Who would have thought sweet, little Bree was a master criminal?" said Candice. She bit into her cookie, and looked fascinated.

"That's exactly why she was so useful to Tom's gang! No one suspected Bree of anything. I don't know what happened between her and Tom. Maybe with the law closing in on them fast, and Tom being so dominating, Bree thought she would grab whatever she could and make a new life for herself away from him. No one knows why she picked Calendar. Detective Logan couldn't find any ties between her and our town. Either she just stumbled across it or she stabbed a finger on the map. It was the perfect place for her to hide out until she could plan for her future." That was all I managed to glean from Detective Logan. He'd been kind enough to keep me updated about his interviews with Tom before his arraignment.

"I heard she was spotted out by that new housing development. Why would she be out there if she didn't intend to stick around?" asked Jaclyn.

I wasn't sure but I had a logical guess. "It's possible Bree might have been looking for a new place to hide the jewels. The realtor said Bree also inquired about buying a house there. The cost would have been chump change after what she stole. Maybe she wanted to find a more secure location to hide her stash; or perhaps she really did want to put down roots here and figure out how to launder the money, instead of running away to somewhere exotic."

"She could hardly explain buying one of those big houses on an assistant librarian's salary," pointed out Candice.

"I'm sure she could have come up with something more convincing. Maybe an inheritance," I suggested. I doubted we'd ever know. Bree didn't tell anyone about her future plans. She was as careful as she could be. The only mistake she made was to use her cellphone before she ditched it, allowing Tom to track her. A little part of me, the part that still considered Bree my friend, hoped that she'd found a happy home here, and that she might have wanted to stay and clean up her life. However, that didn't sit too well with the part of me that knew her as a practiced criminal and confidence trickster.

Despite all that, I couldn't believe every single thing she ever said to me was a lie. Another thing that puzzled me was that Bree never needed anything from me. She could have hidden the jewels in the library at any time. She didn't even have to work there. She also didn't need to cozy up to me to do that. "I'm sure Detective Logan will find out more about both Bree and Tom when he contacts the other police departments," I continued.

"It must have been terrible to realize you were dating a murderer," said my mother. "Although he is good looking..."

I rolled my eyes. Trust my mother to look at any situation with cheerful optimism. "With Bree dead, he had to find someone close to Bree to know if she revealed any information about her past life or the jewels' whereabouts. He intimated that he'd been watching the library for a little while so he knew who I was and that we were friendly. I'm pretty sure he was the one who broke into her apartment but didn't find anything before he decided to target me. He managed to introduce himself and subtly questioned me, checking to see if Bree had confided in me. She hadn't, of course."

"The woman arrested outside my house was part of his gang," chipped in Mom.

I nodded. "She was. Tom realized he wasn't getting anywhere fast so he sent a fake sister to contact me, hoping that I would reveal some information to her instead. I did, but not what they needed. They ended up on a wild goose chase out to Bayview."

"How did you know it was him?" asked Meredith. She warmed her hands on the mug and waited. "That's why we escaped our dates that night, wasn't it?"

I nodded. "I recognized the tattoo on his wrist from one I'd seen in Bree's meager possessions," I said, skipping over the details about going to her former apartment. "It's winter, so everyone wears sweaters, and covers their arms. When Tom pushed his sleeves up to play pool, I saw the tattoo and realized exactly who he was. After that, it wasn't hard to work out why he was taking such an interest in me. When he pulled a gun on me, that clinched it!"

Jaclyn laid a hand on my arm. "It's hard to find a good man these days," she said, her face looking sympathetic. "Thank goodness I have my Donald."

"Your Donald is a cat," said Mom.

"Exactly," agreed Jaclyn. "Dependable."

"Where is Tom now?" asked Meredith. "I hope he gets what's coming to him!"

"I think I can answer that," said a voice behind me. I turned around, smiling when I saw Detective Logan. He nodded politely to my friends and helpers. I wasn't sure if I were mistaken but his eyes seemed to linger on Meredith. "Tom Nicholson is sitting in jail. The judge refused to set bail because he's a flight risk; so he'll stay there until a court date is set. Given the long list of crimes he's purported to have committed, he'll be in the slammer for a long time."

"Good," I said, because it seemed like the simplest answer.

"Have you got a moment?" Detective Logan asked me.

I looked around. We'd almost completed all the packing so I nodded. "Sure," I said. "Let's go into my office."

As we walked away, the group broke into excited conversation, speculating on Tom's fate. I also thought about it a lot over the past week but hadn't gotten much further than hoping he remained inside a jail cell for a very long time. For all of Bree's faults, she didn't deserve to die so unjustly or so cruel.

"What can I help you with?" I asked. "Looking for a new book?"

Detective Logan laughed. "No, but I was thinking I should renew my membership card. I have something for you." He held out a small, black pouch, dropping it into my palm.

"What is it?" I asked.

"Open it up and see."

I slid open the velvet cord and tipped the pouch upside down. Something small and sparkly fell into my hand. I pinched it between thumb and forefinger and held it up, letting the light catch it. "Is this what I think it is?" I asked.

"A diamond," confirmed Detective Logan. "The jewelers were so pleased at the swift recovery of all the jewels that they insisted I give this to you since you were responsible for finding them. It was couriered over this morning."

"It's spectacularly beautiful!" I breathed, utterly astounded at the generous gift.

"I don't think it's the biggest of the recovery but I'm guessing it's worth a small fortune. You deserve it," said Detective Logan. "I have to get back to the station and inform every trespasser we arrested in the past twenty-four hours that there's really no further need to dig for buried treasure now."

"They're still doing that?" I rolled my eyes.

"Yep," said Detective Logan, breaking into a smile that lit his face with warmth. "Take care and try to stay out of trouble."

"I'm just a librarian," I told him. I was still smiling as the detective left the office. I heard him trying to skirt several probing questions from my mother on his way out. I figured he would be fielding those questions for a long time.

"Hey," said Jason, stopping in the doorway. "Meredith told me you were back here. Are you ready?"

"Almost finished," I replied, crossing the few steps between us and reaching up to kiss him as I hooked my arms around his neck. Jason wrapped his arms around my waist, pulling me closer and deepening the kiss. When the kiss ended, his arms remained around me. "How's work at Bayview?" I asked. I was really happy to see him and even happier that we were now on the same team.

"Construction has restarted and we just confirmed the new schedule for completion. Plus, Gwendolyn sold six more homes off plan thanks to the new designs. Did I mention the good press we got for regenerating the library? My firm is very happy about that."

"Did you pick your house?" I wondered. Jason was seriously interested in purchasing a house nearby. He decided he wanted to spend a lot more time in town. I was pretty sure our dates might have influenced his decision. No, I wasn't pretty sure. I was one hundred percent sure. Jason confessed it to me over dinner a few nights ago.

"I did. Do you want to see it?"

"Does it have any walls yet?"

"Might be missing a few."

"Windows? A roof?"

"All currently invisible. I thought I might take you somewhere a little more visible after I show you the large pile of dirt where my house will eventually stand. Do you have your weekend bag?"

"Right here," I said, pointing to my carry-on, which was currently resting by the door. Jason released me, grabbed the handle, and held out his arm for me to hook my own through. "Where are we going?"

"I thought we'd spend the weekend at my apartment in the city and do all those things you keep saying you want to do. Things like going to the theater, doing a little shopping, having romantic dinners. Maybe some tourist sites. Any of that appeal to you?"

I confirmed that it appealed to me very much. "We just need to make a little stop on the way," I told him.

"Where's that?"

"I know a little place that's kind of out of the way, but they make the best pancakes."

Jason threw his head back and laughed. "Let's go!"

I handed my key to my mother, laughing as she all but pushed me out the door. I reminded her to set the new alarm and make sure the door was locked when she left. The next time I saw the inside of the library, it would be fully refurbished. We stepped outside and Jason held up an umbrella, sheltering us both from the rain. Fat droplets hit the ground, reminding me of the unexpected gift Detective Logan had just given me.

"Detective Logan came by," I told him.

"I saw him leaving as I arrived. Did he have good news?"

"Very good." I smiled and held out the diamond for Jason to inspect. "It looks like I got to keep some of the treasure after all!"

If you enjoyed your visit to Calendar, get the next standalone mystery, Fear in February, out in paperback and ebook now!

Ally McKellar loves owning and running her own restaurant, Belle Rose. After working in a busy New York restaurant, managing her own kitchen is like a breath of fresh air. Even better, it's rapidly becoming the local favorite place to go in the quaint, mountain town of Calendar. But if people knew about Ally's recent past, her customers might not be so keen to sample her delicious dishes.

When the local newspaper's food critic makes a reservation to try out her new menu, Ally knows she's got to nail every course to ensure good publicity. There's only one problem: the critic dies during the second course and everything points towards food poisoning. Suddenly, Ally's success as an entrepreneur is in jeopardy while her past is hastily dredged up, threatening to destroy the new life she has recently managed to create.

With the help of Jack Harper, her handsome sous chef with a questionable past of his own, Ally must discover the real killer or risk losing not only Belle Rose, but her desire for a happy new life as well.

Love mysteries? Try Armed & Fabulous, book one in the bestselling Lexi Graves Mysteries, out in paperback and ebook now!

All Lexi wants to do is get through the day at her boring temp job with Green Hand Insurance. That's until she finds the CEO, Martin Dean, in a pool of blood and finds herself at the center of an investigation into insurance fraud.

Millions of dollars are missing, the chief suspect is dead and her mysterious, sexy, new boss is not what he seems.

Recruited by the joint task force working on the case, all Lexi has to do is work out who killed Martin and where the missing millions are. That's easier said than done when her sister is demanding the baby shower to end all baby showers, her wise ass cop family just wants to keep her safe, someone is leaving her creepy gifts and all their clues are leading them to a seedy sex club on the wrong side of town.

As the bodies start to pile up, Lexi is on a race against time to find the killer and the money, before she's next in the murderer's sights.

Made in the USA
Columbia, SC
05 August 2019